Is there anything more glorious than the sight of Luke Callaghan? Oops, I touched a sensitive spot there, since Luke Callaghan was temporarily blinded on his adventures in Mezcaya. But now he's back and he's better than ever! No, I'm not overcompensating for the time in high school when I put hair removal gel in Luke's shampoo. Believe me, he retaliated. I'll just say the words "garden slug" and "daddy longlegs" and that's enough to relay a bad sleeping bag experience during sophomore year camp-out.

Because we're among friends, I can say that Daisy Parker is more twitchy than Mrs. Pritchett's squawking parrot. I haven't been able to get a peep out of Daisy, though she's appreciated my superfudge brownies (bribery). When I tell her that confession is good for the soul, she laughs in my face (although it could

be my new hair color). If anyone knows Daisy's big secret, please let me know. I've had sleepless nights over this one.

And we must keep baby Lena in our thoughts and prayers. She's gone through so much in the last year, and now to be kidnapped! I've been practicing my kickboxing, so, Mr. FBI Agent, Sean Collins, I am ready to be a part of your squad in Operation: Rescue Lena!

Make the Lone Star Country Club your afternoon delight, morning, noon and night....

About the Author

MERLINE LOVELACE

spent twenty-three years in the air force, pulling tours in Vietnam, at the Pentagon and at bases all over the world. When she hung up her uniform, she decided to try her hand at writing. She's since had over forty novels published, with more than five million copies of her works in print.

Merline was thrilled to participate in the LONE STAR COUNTRY CLUB series. She served three different tours of duty in Texas, which is where she met her own handsome hero of thirty-plus years. As a result, the Lone Star State will always hold a special place in her heart.

Watch for Merline's next sizzling, action-packed release. *The Captain's Woman*, featuring Teddy Roosevelt and the Rough Riders, is a January 2003 release from MIRA Books.

MERLINE LOVELACE

TEXAS...NOW AND FOREVER

Silhouette Books

Published by Silhouette Books

America's Publisher of Contemporary Romance

Special thanks and acknowledgment are given to Merline Lovelace for her contribution to the LONE STAR COUNTRY CLUB series.

 SILHOUETTE BOOKS

ISBN 0-373-61363-6

TEXAS...NOW AND FOREVER

Visit Silhouette at www.eHarlequin.com

Printed in U.S.A.

Welcome to the

*Where Texas society reigns supreme—
and appearances are everything.*

Danger reaches a fever pitch in Mission Creek....

Luke Callaghan: The Lone Star Country Club elite couldn't spread the news fast enough that one of their own—international millionaire Luke Callaghan—was baby Lena's flesh-and-blood daddy! But against all odds could this battle-scarred war hero save his tyke from a deadly foe?

Haley Mercado: After receiving a menacing call from her daughter's kidnapper to do his bidding—or else!—she had no choice but to come out of hiding and enlist the help of her former flame, Luke Callaghan, if she ever wanted to see her baby alive again. But could their love—and his specialized military training—triumph over peril, heartache...and the ultimate betrayal?

Miracle in Mission Creek: The entire town bands together as explosive revelations send shock waves through Mission Creek...and the search for baby Lena reaches a shattering climax. But will it take a miracle to end the bitter feud between the Carsons and the Wainwrights?

THE FAMILIES

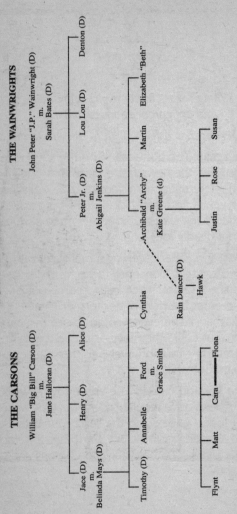

THE CARSONS

William "Big Bill" Carson (D)
m.
Jane Halloran (D)

- Jace (D)
  m.
  Belinda Mays (D)
- Henry (D)
- Alice (D)

- Timothy (D)
  m.
  Annabelle

- Ford
  m.
  Grace Smith
- Cynthia

- Flynt
- Matt
- Cara ═══ Fiona

THE WAINWRIGHTS

John Peter "J.P." Wainwright (D)
m.
Sarah Bates (D)

- Peter Jr. (D)
  m.
  Abigail Jenkins (D)
- Lou Lou (D)
- Denton (D)

- Archibald "Archy"
  m.
  Kate Greene (d)
- Martin
- Elizabeth "Beth"

- Justin
- Rose
- Susan

Rain Dancer (D)
Hawk

D   Deceased
d   Divorced
m.   Married
- - - Affair
═══ Twins

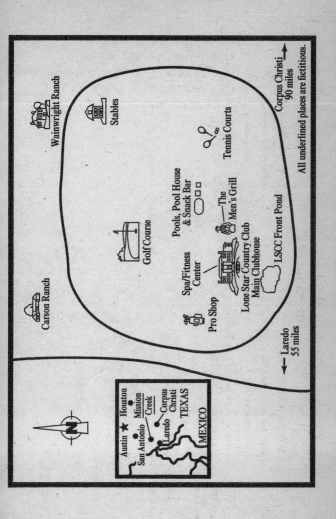

Wainwright Ranch

Carson Ranch

Stables

Tennis Courts

Golf Course

Pools, Pool House
& Snack Bar

The
Men's Grill

Spa/Fitness
Center

Lone Star Country Club
Main Clubhouse

LSCC Front Pond

Pro Shop

← Laredo
55 miles

Corpus Christi
90 miles →

All underlined places are fictitious.

Austin ★ Houston
Mission
San Antonio Creek
Corpus Christi
Laredo
TEXAS
MEXICO

N

For my own handsome hero,
and all the days and nights
we spent under Texas skies during our assignments
in Fort Worth and San Antonio.
Thanks for the memories, my darling.

One

A shrill buzz cut through the air-conditioned silence, haunting the small farmhouse just outside Mission Creek, Texas. Like a deer speared by truck headlights, Haley Mercado froze. Her glance sliced to the FBI agent who'd acted as her controller for the past year.

Across the living room Sean Collins met her desperate look. They'd been waiting for this call, she and Sean. So had the small army of agents guarding the safe house where the FBI had stashed Haley until they captured Frank Del Brio.

Frank Del Brio. The smooth, handsome head of the Texas mob who'd once shoved a square-cut, three-carat diamond on Haley's finger and announced that she was going to marry him. The ruthless thug who'd forced her to flee her home in South Texas and to assume another identity abroad. The vicious killer whose horrific acts had brought Haley out of hiding a year ago and sent her undercover, determined to assist the FBI in bringing Del Brio down.

Frank Del Brio, who'd kidnapped the child she'd placed in safekeeping while she worked undercover, the child who only a few nights ago had been spared in a wild shoot-out that had left her father in ICU and Haley under close protection at this secluded farmhouse.

The phone shrilled again, sending a jolt of desperate hope into her chest. They've got him! Please, God! Please let this call be from the FBI command center, advising that they've cornered Frank and rescued her baby! Her heart in her throat, she wiped her palms down the front of her jeans and kept her gaze locked on Sean as he reached for the cordless phone.

"Collins here."

When the FBI operative's face tightened, Haley's hope shattered into a thousand knife-edged shards.

"How the hell did you get this number?"

It was Frank, she thought on a wave of sickening certainty. It could only be Frank.

Collins confirmed it in the next breath. "No way I'm putting her on the phone, Del Brio. You can damned well talk to me."

The mobster's response sent a tide of angry red surging into the FBI agent's cheeks. His eyes blazing fire, Sean snarled back.

"Listen to me, you two-bit piece of slime. You

hurt that baby and there won't a patch of dirt any-where on this earth big enough for you to dig a hole and crawl into.''

Haley flew across the living room. "Let me talk to him.''

"I'm warning you, Del Brio—''

"Let me talk to him!''

The agent relinquished the instrument reluc-tantly, signaling for Haley to string out the con-versation as long as she could. She understood. The communications technicians hooked into the line would need a few moments to trace the call. She understood, too, that the events of the past year were rapidly spiraling to a terrifying conclusion.

"Frank! Frank, are you there?''

"Hello, Daisy.''

The deep, rich baritone made her skin crawl.

"You fooled me with that brassy hair and nose job, babe, but I have to admit I like the new look.''

Haley didn't bother to comment on the fact that he'd penetrated the cover she'd been using for the past year. The long months she'd spent as Daisy Parker didn't matter anymore. All that mattered was her baby. Only her baby.

"Don't hurt her, Frank. Please, don't hurt her.''

She hated to beg, hated hearing the abject plead-ing in her voice, almost as much as she hated Del Brio for the pain he'd caused her and her family.

"What do you want?" she whispered. "What do I have to do to get Lena back?"

"Two million just might do the trick. In unmarked, nonsequential bills. Nothing bigger than a hundred. I'll let you know where and when to deliver it."

His voice dropped to a low caress. Soft and husky, it scraped across Haley's raw nerves like a rusty nail.

"I'd better not see one cop or one fed, particularly your pal Collins or that bastard Justin Wainwright."

Haley's heart squeezed with pain. They'd come so close, so very close. Mission Creek's sheriff and the FBI had almost—almost—captured Del Brio three nights ago. He'd made his escape, gunning down her father in the process. Taking her baby with him.

"If I even smell their stink when you deliver the ransom," Frank snarled, "you'll never see your brat again. You understand me?"

"Yes."

"Good. Talk to you soon, babe."

"Wait!" Her frantic shout bounced off the walls. "Don't hang up! Tell me how she's—"

The hum of the disconnected line thundered in Haley's ear. She wanted to scream, to shriek and batter the receiver against the phone. But she'd spent the past year living a dangerous lie. A year undercover, risking her life every day to ferret out the details of the mob that had operated out of Mission Creek. If nothing else, those torturous months had taught her to subdue every natural impulse. To smile when she shook inside with fear. To hide her anguish as she watched another couple love and cherish the baby she'd been forced to give up temporarily for the child's own safety.

All those months had left their mark on Haley. Instead of shrieking or hurling the cordless phone at the wall, she merely handed it to Sean and listened in stony silence while he barked at the communications techs working the trace.

"Did you pinpoint the location?"

She knew. Even before she saw his mouth twist into a disgusted grimace, she knew. Frank was too smart to trip himself up with a simple phone call.

"Okay. Thanks."

His jaw tight, Sean punched the off button. Frustration gave a sharp edge to his broad New York accent when he confirmed what she already suspected.

"Del Brio used some kind of electronic scrambler. We couldn't confirm his location."

She nodded. That was all she could manage. From the day Lena was kidnapped, Haley had carried both fear and dread around inside her like a stone. It crushed in on her now, so massive and heavy she could hardly breathe.

"He'll kill her."

"Listen to me, Daisy—"

The special agent caught himself. He'd insisted they use her alias of Daisy Parker in every communication and every conversation for the past year. Although that cover was now blown, Sean hadn't quite made the transition back to her real name.

"Listen to me, Haley. Del Brio can't kill Lena. Not until he gets what he wants. He knows we'll demand proof she's still alive before we play his game."

The iron control she'd exercised for more than a year slipped and came close to shattering at that moment. "It's not a game!" she snapped furiously. "This is my child's life we're talking about!"

"Dammit, I know that."

Months of unrelenting tension sizzled and spit between them. With a little push Haley could almost have hated Sean Collins, too.

"I'm sorry," he said finally, shagging a hand through his thick, reddish hair. "You know I'll do whatever it takes to get Lena back. I want Del Brio as much as you do."

"No," she countered swiftly, her throat raw. "You couldn't. It wasn't your mother Frank murdered, Sean. Your father he tried to destroy. Your trusted friend and advisor he blew away.''

She closed her eyes, aching for her mother. Grieving for the white-haired Texas judge who'd helped her arrange her escape and acted as her lifeline all those years she stayed in hiding. Hurting, too, for the father who now lay in ICU, battling for every breath.

Frank Del Brio had wreaked such havoc on her life. Haley knew he wouldn't hesitate to take the next fatal step. She wrapped her arms around her middle and squeezed tight, wishing with every ounce of her being she could hold in her terror for her child and keep it from spilling into reality.

Eyes closed, she pictured Lena the last time she'd seen her. The one-year-old was such a happy, bubbly child. All smiles and gurgles and bright blue eyes. With her mother's pointed chin and her father's black curly hair.

Her father. Oh, God! Her father.

Luke Callaghan.

Swallowing the moan that tried to escape, Haley dug her hands into her sides. She had to tell Luke. Had to confirm what the DNA tests had already substantiated. He was Lena's father. When she admitted that, she'd have to confess, too, that the blond waitress he knew as Daisy Parker was Lena's mother.

She cringed at the thought of having to explain to Luke the tangled web of lies and deceit she'd woven to protect herself and Lena, but every instinct told her he was now her only hope. Frank had warned her not to bring the feds when she delivered the ransom. He hadn't said anything about the baby's father.

Her mind worked feverishly. Del Brio was ruthless and totally without conscience. He also exercised an extensive network of contacts. He'd known how to reach Haley here, in this supposedly secure haven. He'd probably get word within minutes if she left it and went to Lena's father. He wouldn't worry, though. If there was a chink in Del Brio's armor, it was his arrogance. He wouldn't doubt his ability to handle the combination of a terrified mother and a blind father.

But could Haley handle it? After all this time, could she face the man who'd fathered her child? The man she'd loved as long as she could remember?

She could.

She had to!

Spinning, she bolted for the front door. Sean followed hard on her heels.

"Where are you going?"

"To find Luke Callaghan."

"No way! You're not setting foot outside this safe house."

"Safe?" Whirling, she leapt to the attack. "What's safe about it? Frank knows where I am. He got through your command center's elaborate electronic screens with one call. If he wanted to, he could probably order one of his goons to launch a shoulder-held missile from a mile away and put it through that window right now."

The fact that they both knew she was right didn't lessen Sean's bulldog stance. "We've made it this far together, Dai—Haley. Don't give up on me now."

"I'm not giving up. I've just decided to play the game by Frank's ground rules." Icy resolve coated every word. "He wants two million dollars. As you pointed out, he's not likely to hurt me or my child until I deliver it. And I do intend to deliver it. With Luke Callaghan."

"Christ! Callaghan's a good man. A war hero, no less. But he can't see a red flag waved two inches in front of his face."

A new ache pierced Haley's heart, adding another layer to the hurt and guilt and fear she'd carried for so long. Seeing the pain on her face, Sean backpedaled gruffly.

"Look, I'll admit Callaghan has moved mountains to help us find Lena. Once DNA tests indicated that he was her father, he let us tap his phones. He offered to provide the ransom, when and if it was demanded. He even volunteered the theory that he was the source the kidnappers intended to milk right from the start. With all his millions, it was certainly a distinct possibility.''

More than a possibility. Since Lena had been taken just days before Luke returned to Mission Creek, everyone on the task force initially suspected his vast wealth had sparked the kidnapping.

''Callaghan also worked his own net,'' the FBI agent conceded with a touch of grudging admiration. ''He has more contacts than any six men I know. And not just in the government. He and those three buddies of his scoured more dives, bribed more drunks and coerced more lowlifes into spilling their guts than our entire task force. But he can't—''

''No buts,'' Haley interjected swiftly, fiercely. ''Luke Callaghan is Lena's father. I can't let him stand idly on the sidelines now while Frank Del Brio barters her for blood money.''

Reaching for the door, she yanked it open. Sean's big, beefy hand smacked hard against the wood panel.

''Don't try to stop me,'' Haley hissed. ''Don't even think about trying to stop me. I've done everything you asked me to, Sean. All these months

I risked my life to provide the information you wanted. I will not risk my child's.''

"All right!" Conceding defeat, the FBI operative nodded. "Hang loose a minute. I'll have my people track Callaghan down for you."

Haley drove away from the farmhouse a few moments later, trailed by a dusty white van and armed with the 9 mm Glock that Sean had instructed one of his agents to hand over.

She knew how to fire the handgun. She'd grown up in this patch of South Texas, on a sprawling acreage just outside Mission Creek. Indulged by her parents and spoiled shamefully by her older brother, Ricky, she'd spent most of her after-school hours in voice lessons, dance classes and giggling with her girlfriends as they checked out the hunks at the pool of the luxurious Lone Star Country Club. Ricky had taken her out to ping tin cans off fence poles often enough for Haley to know one end of a gun from another, though.

Grimly, she locked her hands around the steering wheel and drove through the night. A million stars winked in the inky sky. The moon hung low, dazzling in its silver glow. Haley didn't even spare it a glance.

As promised, Sean had pinpointed Luke Callaghan's present location. He was with one of his buddies. At the Saddlebag. The same watering hole where Haley had bumped into him two years ago, with such earth-shattering consequences.

The irony of seeking Luke out at the Saddlebag ate into her soul. He hadn't recognized her that hot July night two years ago. The London plastic surgeon who'd altered Haley's face had more than earned his five thousand pounds. Luke wouldn't recognize her tonight, either. Not just because he'd lost his sight, but because she'd all but crawled into the skin of the fictional Daisy Parker. No one—until Frank—had penetrated her cover.

Although…

Lately, Luke had been asking questions about the blond waitress with the thick-as-road-tar Texas twang. He'd even cornered her once at the Lone Star Country Club. He'd brushed his mouth across hers, as if testing his memory. He'd tested Haley's nerves, as well. She'd shied away, refusing to admit she knew him.

Now she'd not only admit that she knew him and that she'd had his baby, but she'd grovel at his feet if necessary to gain his help in reclaiming their child.

Her mouth had settled into a determined line when she wheeled into the Saddlebag's jam-packed parking lot some twenty minutes later and nosed her car into the narrow space between two pickups. The white van parked some yards away. At this point Haley couldn't say whether the FBI's watchful vigilance reassured her or added to the stress that crawled across her shoulder blades like a Texas scorpion.

Her throat tight, she climbed out of the car. The Saddlebag hadn't changed much in two years. The same wooden sign creaked in the breeze above the door. The same dim spotlights cast arcs of light against its gray, weathered siding. The same motel units were strung out behind the bar like plump, feathered hens roosting for the night. With a stab of acute pain, Haley wrenched her gaze from the largest of the ten or so units and headed for the bar.

When she pushed through the front door, the country-western music pouring through the wall-mounted speakers competed with the remembered clack of pool balls. Haley stood beside an arch formed by branding irons, hidden in its shadows. Narrowing her eyes, she peered through the blue haze. Establishments in this part of South Texas didn't run to separate smoking sections.

Her gaze skimmed the handful of customers at the long curved bar that wrapped clear around to the back of the lounge. She recognized several patrons. She'd waited on them at the country club. Ignoring the sudden, hopeful gleam in one man's eye and the welcoming wave of another, she turned her attention to the half dozen tables at the rear of the bar.

With a sudden thump of her heart, she spotted two men nursing dew-streaked long-necks at one of the tables. Her glance skimmed past Tyler Murdoch to lock on Luke. His back was to her, but Haley couldn't mistake the curly black hair cut military short under his summer straw Stetson or the athletic shoulders stretching the seams of his blue denim shirt. Every inch of Luke Callaghan's powerful, muscular body was imprinted on her memory.

She'd been in love with him for as long as she could remember. The orphaned son of wealthy parents, Luke had grown up on the Callaghan's lavish estate just north of Mission Creek, cared for by a devoted housekeeper and an absentee uncle not above dipping into his nephew's trust fund to maintain his free-wheeling lifestyle. Luke and Haley's brother had been friends since grade school, then roomed together at V.M.I.—Virginia Military Institute—where Luke and Ricky and three other classmates from the local area had formed their own special clique. The Fabulous Five, Haley had secretly labeled them. A band of brothers so tight and close it seemed that nothing could ever shake their friendship.

Ricky Mercado, the brother she adored.

Flynt Carson, scion of one of the old cattle king families that had settled this corner of South Texas.

Spence Harrison, brown-haired, brown-eyed and all male.

Tyler Murdoch, rugged, rough-edged, with an uncanny flair for anything and everything mechanical.

And Luke. Laughing, blue-eyed Luke Callaghan.

Haley had developed severe crushes on each of her brother's pals at one time or another, but Luke had stolen her heart. She was so young when she'd first tumbled into love with him, just growing into the seductive curves and smoldering Italian looks she'd inherited from her mother. A typical teenage girl, she'd alternated between outrageously blatant attempts to attract Luke's attention and tongue-tied shyness when she did.

He'd been kind to her, she remembered on a wave of stinging regret for those golden days of her girlhood. Teasing and big-brotherly and kind. If he'd recognized the signs of adolescent fixation, he never let on.

During her college years she'd seen Luke less frequently, but each time she did, she'd fallen a little more in love with him. He and Ricky and the others had joined the marines by then. They made only brief trips home for the holidays or lightning-quick visits en route to some mission or another. To Haley's chagrin, Luke didn't spend enough time at home to notice that Ricky's sister was now all grown up.

If he hadn't noticed, however, Frank Del Brio certainly had.

Shuddering, Haley recalled how the handsome older man had started hitting on her soon after her graduation from the University of Texas. It shamed her now to admit that his attentions had flattered her at first. Dark-haired, dark-eyed, and six-two of solid muscle, Frank could charm the knickers off a nun if he wanted to. Only after Haley had come to understand how deeply Del Brio was involved in her uncle Carmine's more dangerous undertakings did she try to break things off.

He'd given her a first taste of his temper then, and of his ruthlessness. Her father was in the family business, too, Frank had reminded Haley with a smile. Not as deep as his brother, Carmine, certainly, but deep enough to make him a target for the feds or for rival mob members if the right hints were dropped in the wrong ears. The threat was still hanging heavy on her mind when Frank slid a diamond ring onto her finger.

Then Ricky and Luke and their friends had volunteered for a highly classified, dangerous mission during the Gulf War. To this day Haley knew only vague details of that mission. Her brother never talked about it. Nor did any of the other four. All she knew was that they'd been dropped behind enemy lines, destroyed a biological weapons manufacturing plant, were captured and spent agonizing months as POWs until their commander, Phillip Westin, mounted a daring rescue raid.

The Fabulous Five came home to a hero's welcome. Haley would never forget the parade held in their honor one blazing June morning. Or their wild, lakeside celebration that night.

That was the night Haley Mercado died.

Two

More than a decade earlier

"Guys! Hey, guys!"

Waving wildly, Haley shouted to the occupants of the powerful speedboat cutting across Lake Maria.

"Luke! Ricky! Over here, darn it!"

With a disgusted huff that lifted the tendrils of her mink-brown hair, Haley gave it up as hopeless. The long shadows creeping across the lake had reached the dock. They couldn't see her, and she knew they couldn't hear her above the engine's roar.

Retreating to the sleek little two-seater sports car she'd parked at the head of the pier, she groped for the headlight switch. It took several bright flashes, but she finally caught the boaters's attention. The man at the wheel waved, leaned right and brought the craft into a sharp turn.

Haley drifted back down to the dock to await its arrival. Her brother, Ricky, and his four buddies had been water-skiing all afternoon, slicing through the water with reckless abandon. She could certainly understand their craving to feel the sun and the wind on their skin.

They'd more than earned these hours on the lake, considering the morning they'd just put in. From nine o'clock on, the returning POWs had been on display. After all, folks around here considered them gen-u-ine Texas heroes, not to mention poster ads for the United States Marine Corps. Spit-shined, square-shouldered, and heart-stoppingly handsome in their uniforms, they'd ridden in the parade organized in their honor. Then, of course, they'd had to sit under the hot sun, steaming in their high-collared dress blues, while local dignitaries gave long-winded speeches about South Texas's own. They'd even signed autographs for the kids who'd swarmed the platform after the speeches.

The minute the crowds had dispersed, however, they'd shed their decorum along with their uniforms and headed for the lake. They'd been here for a good five hours, tossing down beer and celebrating their hard-won freedom. The sun was now a flaming ball hanging low above the hills surrounding Lake Maria. If they didn't come in and dry off soon, they'd be navigating in the dark. More to the point, they'd miss the lavish barbecue

Isadora and Johnny Mercado were throwing at their lakeside cottage to welcome Ricky and his friends home.

Leaning her hips against a piling, Haley peered across the rippling water at the approaching boat. Her heart contracted painfully as she made out the features of the man at the wheel. Luke Callaghan stood wide-legged and strong, his bare chest glistening in the slanting rays of the sun. Leathertough Tyler Murdoch sat beside him. Although she couldn't make out the figures in the back of the boat, she knew their faces as well as her own. Tooserious Flynt Carson. Intense, intent Spence Harrison. And Ricky, Haley's adored older brother.

Thank God they'd all made it back safely, she thought on a wave of bone-deep relief. With their return, at least one of the worries that had kept her sleepless and hollow-eyed these past weeks had been allayed. The other...

The other she'd take care of tonight.

Her stomach clenching, Haley glanced down at the square-cut diamond on her left hand. The enormity of what she planned to do just a few hours from now started nausea churning in her stomach.

Damn Frank Del Brio!

The speedboat's throaty roar brought her head up. Squinting, she watched as Luke brought the powerful machine skimming toward the dock.

With consummate skill, he throttled back mere yards from the pier, reversed thrust on the dual engines and floated the craft up to the pilings. The man sprawled beside Luke grinned up at her as she caught their line.

"Hey, sweet thing."

"Hey, Tyler."

The former all-conference wide receiver skimmed an appreciative glance from her shoulders, left bare by the red-checked halter top tied just below her full breasts, to the long legs showing beneath her red linen shorts.

"You're looking good tonight."

"Thanks."

Luke appeared to share his opinion. Haley's skin prickled as his gaze made a slow pass from her neck to her knees. But when he addressed her, his voice held the same carelessly affectionate tone he always used with his best buddy's little sister.

"Want to go for a spin?"

"I wish I could," she said with real longing. The water looked so dark and green and cool, and Luke so sleek and powerful in his wet swimming trunks. Wrenching her gaze from his broad chest and flat belly, Haley searched the back of the boat for her brother.

"Where's Ricky?"

"We dropped him off at the marina about fifteen

minutes ago. He said he had to pick up Melissa
and take her to the party your folks are throwing
for us.''

''Well, shoot!''

''Is that a problem?''

''No, not really. Melissa called the house a half
hour ago, asking where he was. Like a good sister,
I drove all the way around the lake to fetch him.
Now I'll have to drive all the way back.''

She glanced across the wide expanse of water.
The lights the Mercados had strung in the backyard
of their lakeside cottage in preparation for the barbecue winked like lightning bugs in the gathering
dusk. Those pinpricks of light punched a fist-size
hole in Haley's heart.

Isadora Mercado had thrown herself into arrang-
ing this party. It looked to be one of the biggest
events of the year. A joyous celebration. A gathering of all Ricky's and Luke's friends beneath a
star-filled Texas sky.

Only Isadora's daughter—and Judge Carl
Bridges—knew it would be the last night Haley
Mercado would spend with her family. The last
hours she'd share with her friends.

The last moments she'd have with Luke.

Her right hand closed over her left with bruising
force. The edges of the diamond gouged into the

undersides of her fingers. Frank Del Brio was to blame—for everything.

"We were just planning to head across the lake to the party ourselves," Luke said, cutting into her chaotic thoughts. "Why don't you come with us? It'll save you the long drive."

"No, I... I can't."

Haley would go out on these dark waters soon enough. When she did, she wouldn't come back in.

"Sure you can," Spence Harrison countered from his seat behind Luke's. "Haul your butt back here, Tyler, and make room for the lady."

She shook her head. "I need my car."

Her sporty little vehicle represented an integral element of the plan she and Judge Bridges had worked out. Haley would slip away from the party once it was in full swing. Drive to a secluded cove on this very lake. Leave the coverup to her bathing suit on the front seat. Go for a late-night swim. Disappear forever.

"You can retrieve the car tomorrow," sandy-haired Flynt Carson put in. "Better climb in, kid, or you'll miss the festivities."

Haley's glance darted to Luke. The urge to spend just a few more minutes with him pulled at her like talons dug deep into her heart. She'd never see him again after tonight. Never know if the lazy glances he'd sent her way in the past year or so might have developed into something deeper, something that had nothing to do with the brotherly affection he always showed her.

Misinterpreting the reason for her hesitation, Luke cocked a brow. ''Are you thinking we've downed too much beer to get you safely across the lake? Don't worry about the open cans littering the back of the boat. We're big boys. We knew we were getting close to our limit. To avoid temptation, we emptied the last couple of six packs over the side right after we dropped Ricky off. You're safe with us, Haley.''

Oh, God. If only that were true!

''Here.'' Smiling, Luke held up his hand. ''I'll help you in.''

The fierce desire to slip her hand into his sliced through Haley. Frantically her mind raced to revise her carefully laid plans. She'd leave her car here and borrow one of her parents' when it was time to sneak away from the party. Then, she could take this last boat ride with Ricky's friends and steal another few moments with Luke.

Her hand eased into his. His grip was strong and sure and wet from the spray as he helped her into the boat. Once she'd found her footing, he held her fingers up to the light. Turning her hand from one side to the other, he studied her ring. The multifaceted diamond caught the last rays of the sun. Brightly colored sparks leapt from her hand.

Luke had seen the ring before, of course. Haley had been wearing it like a brand since the day he and Ricky and the others had returned home. This was the first time he'd examined it up close, however.

"That's some rock," he commented with a grin.

"Yes." Her response was flat and lacking any emotion. "It is."

"Funny," he murmured, searching her face, "I never saw you and Frank Del Brio as a match."

"Funny," Haley got out in a strangled voice, "neither did I."

What a fool she'd been! What a naive, idiotic fool! She'd been so convinced she could turn aside Frank's increasingly ardent demands. So sure he would understand when she told him she just didn't feel the same passion he seemed to feel for her.

He'd make her feel it, Frank had insisted. Make her love him. All she had to do was give him a chance. And remember how much he knew about her father's involvement with the fringes of the mob.

Haley had agreed to the engagement in a desperate attempt to buy time. Now that time was about to run out. With her supposed wedding day rapidly approaching, she'd realized that the only way she could save her father—and save herself—was to disappear. Permanently.

Which she intended to do tonight.

But first she'd spend these few last moments with Luke, she decided fiercely.

"Want to take the wheel?" he offered.

"Of this behemoth?" She forced a smile. "I don't know if I've got the strength to muscle her all the way across the lake."

"No sweat. I'll act as your backup."

Positioning Haley at the wheel, he stationed himself behind her and worked the throttles. Slowly the high-powered speedboat backed away from the dock. Once it was clear, Haley brought its nose around. Luke's deep drawl sounded just above her ear.

"Ready?"

His warm breath sent shivers rippling along her bare shoulders. "Ready."

"Okay, let's open her up."

He shoved the throttles forward. With the snarl of an oversize jungle cat, the engine revved. The speedboat shot straight ahead. The hull lifted half out of the water, came down with a sharp crack, then rocketed across the surface.

The forward thrust knocked Haley against Luke. Legs spread wide, he grabbed the edge of the windshield to steady himself and to give her added support. With the wheel close against her front and Luke hard against her back, there wasn't room for Haley to pull away, even if she wanted to.

Spray flew into her face. The wind whipped her hair around like hissing snakes until Luke laughed and caught the flying strands. Holding them in his fist, he rested his hand on her shoulder. Haley forced herself to relax and to lean against him. Keeping the nose of the boat aimed at the lights winking on the far shore, she fought a sliver of pure pain.

How many times had she fantasized about Luke holding her like this? How many nights had she fallen asleep aching for the feel of his warm, hard flesh against hers? How often had she wished he would lock his arms around her and make her forget the rest of the world?

Now, at this minute, she'd come as close to realizing her dream as she ever would. Closing her eyes, she tried to burn the imprint of his body into her memory. Her senses recorded the clean, lake-washed scent of his skin. The way her head fit perfectly into the muscled curve of his shoulder. The bulge of hard masculinity nudging her behind.

"Haley! Watch out for that submerged log!"

Her eyes flew open, locked for a second or two on the glowing lights, then dropped to the water's surface. Shocked by the sight of a thick weathered branch on the lake dead ahead, she threw the boat into a turn. The right gunwale went down, slicing deep into the dark water. The left rose high into the air. The high-powered speedboat raced on with water sloshing into its deck well and five startled occupants all scrambling for a handhold.

Shoving her aside, Luke dived for the wheel. The movement destroyed Haley's already shaky balance. She made a frantic grab for the windshield, the seat, anything to anchor her, but her flailing, spray-slick hands found nothing but empty air. With a little cry, she tumbled over the side.

"Haley!"

Luke's shout was the last sound she heard before she sank into the water. She plunged downward, her movements jerky and uncoordinated until she conquered her momentary panic. She'd spent hours as a toddler dog-paddling in this lake. Many more as a youngster jet-skiing and water-skiing across its vast surface. The lake was her friend.

Her escape.

Tucking her legs, she righted herself and shot toward the surface. Her ascent was as smooth as her descent had been wild and tumultuous. For the first second or two, anyway.

She was still four or five feet below the surface when something scraped along her neck and jerked her to a halt. Fright almost stripped the last of her air from her lungs. Thrashing, twisting, she fought a long tentacle of the submerged tree she'd swerved to avoid. The tip of the branch had slipped right under the neck strap of her halter. Her body's buoyancy and her own frantic movements kept the damned thing securely lodged.

Her chest burning, Haley tore at the knot tied just under her breasts. Air bubbles were escaping her aching lungs by the time the knot finally gave. Abandoning the scrap of fabric, she scissor-kicked frantically. She burst through the surface a second later. Gasping, choking, she dragged in huge gulps of air.

When she gathered her strength enough to make a quick spin, what she saw almost sucked the air right back out of her lungs.

''Dear God!''

She felt as though she'd been under water for hours, but it must have been only a few seconds. Not long enough for Luke to regain control of the speedboat, which now tipped even more precariously to one side. Water flew up in white sheets as it cut a crazy swath toward the flickering lights.

''Luke! Tyler!'' Treading water, Haley screamed a desperate warning. ''Flynt, she's going to flip. Get the heck out of there, guys!''

They were too far away now to hear her shout.

Or too busy throwing their weight against the up-raised side. The maneuver might have worked on a sailboat tacking into the wind. On a speedboat with one of its dual engines still churning at full power, it had little effect.

As Haley squinted through the darkening shadows, horrified, the fiberglass hull raised even higher. A second later the entire boat went over and hit with a crack that rifled across the lake like gunfire. Her heart stayed lodged firmly in her throat until she saw dark shapes bob to the surface.

One. Two. Three.

Where was the fourth? Oh, God, where was the fourth!

She kicked, launching into a desperate stroke, but knew she'd never cover the distance that now yawned between her and the men thrown from the speedboat to do any good. They were closer to the far shore than they were to her. The people running down to the pier of her parents' lakeside cabin would reach the capsized boat long before she could.

Still, she swam doggedly, desperately, until a fourth dark shape broke the surface. Half choking, half sobbing with relief, Haley slowed her stroke until she was again treading water.

They couldn't see her, she realized, when she shoved her wet hair out of her eyes. The last, dying rays of the sun illuminated the far shore, but shadows were deeper out here. Darker. None of the figures on the far shore could spot her from that distance.

But they'd come looking for her. As soon as they reached Luke and the others and learned Haley had been in the boat, too, they'd come in search of her. Her father. Her brother.

Frank Del Brio.

The heat generated by Haley's frenetic swim evaporated. Ice crystals seemed to form in her veins. Her arms grew as heavy as the gray granite boulders lining the shore, her heart even heavier.

She'd intended to disappear tonight. Not in such a dramatic manner, perhaps, but... Well, a drowning was a drowning.

She swallowed. Hard. With little finning movements with her hands, she brought her body around. The closest spit of land was a hundred or so yards away. Several miles from the secluded cove where she'd planned to park her car to go for her last swim, but within walking distance of the judge's isolated fishing cabin.

Judge Carl Bridges. The one man she could trust. The lawyer who'd been both longtime friend to her family and calm advisor to an increasingly desperate Haley. With his cloak of client-attorney privilege, the judge knew how deeply Johnny Mercado had become entangled in his brother Carmine's deadly web. He also knew that Frank Del Brio's threats were anything but idle. He suspected the smooth, handsome thug of complicity in several vicious killings. He understood Haley's wrenching decision to protect her father in the only way she could—by removing herself completely from the equation. If she was gone, Frank would have no reason to threaten her father.

During the past weeks the judge had obtained a forged passport and purchased airline tickets that would send Haley crisscrossing three continents and, hopefully, cover her tracks from even the most determined scrutiny. Everything was ready. Tonight was the night. And, with this bizarre boating accident, she'd never have a better opportunity to make her death look real.

Her heart splintering, Haley threw a last look over her shoulder. In a ragged whisper she said goodbye to her home and to her family.

"I love you, Mom," she whispered. "You and Daddy both. Keep safe, and keep Ricky safe."

Dragging off Frank's engagement ring, she threw it as far as she could. Then she slipped beneath the cool, dark waters once more.

Three

Half-naked and totally exhausted, Haley dragged herself out of the lake. She didn't look back. She didn't dare.

Twenty minutes later she stumbled down the path to a small, ramshackle fishing cabin tucked among a stand of scrub pine. No lights showed at the shuttered windows. The judge hadn't yet arrived at the agreed-upon rendezvous site. But he would. Soon, she guessed.

Once inside the back door Carl Bridges always kept unlocked, she grabbed a blue plaid flannel shirt from the hooks on the wall and hunched on one of the sturdy chairs drawn up to the scarred plank table.

The immensity of what she'd just done—and what she was about to do—almost overwhelmed her. Shaking from head to toe, she wrapped her arms around her middle and rocked back and forth. Lake water dripped from her hair and ran down her legs to puddle on the scrubbed pine floor.

She done it. She'd completed the first phase of

her plan. Not the way she and the judge had en-
visioned it, precisely, but the speedboat accident
would certainly make things more realistic. Now
she just had to find the courage to take the next
step. Could she really put her parents through the
agony of believing she'd drowned? Really leave
Texas and start a new life, away from everything
and everyone she knew?

Away from Frank?

With a little moan, Haley dug her fingers into
her sides. She had no choice. Frank would destroy
her father. He was that determined. And that vicious.

She'd find a way to let her parents know she
was okay, she swore. Later, when she was sure it
was safe.

The thought gave her the strength to make it
through the wait for Judge Bridges. As an old and
trusted friend of the family, he'd been invited to
celebrate the boys' homecoming. He would have
been one of the crowd gathered under the flickering lights. One of the witnesses to the accident out
on the lake. When Luke and the others made it
known Haley had been a passenger in the boat,
Carl would guess that she'd altered the schedule.

Sure enough, tires crunched on the dirt-and-
gravel road leading to the cabin less than a half
hour later. Haley was a bundle of raw nerves, but

her rapidly developing self-preservation instinct kept her out of sight as she peered through the bedroom window. She almost wept with relief when Judge Bridges slammed the car door. His prematurely white hair shining like a beacon in the darkness that now blanketed the earth, he rushed to the cabin.

"Haley? Haley, are you here?"

"Yes!" She ran in from the other room. "Yes, I'm here."

"Thank God!"

His lined face was a study in worry and relief. Opening his arms, he crushed her against his chest. Haley clung to him with everything in her. He was her last link with her family. The last link between the woman she was and the stranger she would soon become.

Finally his hold loosened. He eased her away a few inches. "I thought… We all thought…"

His Adam's apple bobbed up and down. Behind his old-fashioned black-rimmed glasses, his watery blue eyes glistened. Blinking furiously, he glared at her with a combination of anger and admiration.

"Why the dickens did you flip over Luke's speedboat? That was a dangerous stunt and not part of our plan."

"I didn't flip it! Well, I guess I did, but not on

purpose. I swerved to avoid a submerged log and lost control.''

''Well, it sure adds a grim authenticity to our plan. They're searching the whole lake for you, missy.''

''Oh, Judge!'' Wracked with guilt, Haley almost abandoned the scheme right then and there. ''My parents must be frantic. Maybe I should go home. Maybe I should just marry Frank.''

Her tortured doubts acted like a spur on the judge. The steely resolve that had sustained him through fifteen years at the bar and ten on the bench stiffened his spine.

''No, Haley, you're doing the right thing. You've got to get away. Your parents did everything they could to give you and Ricky a different life. If you go back now, you'll nullify all their years of sacrifice and worry.''

She knew he was right. Carl Bridges had been both friend and advisor to Johnny and Isadora Mercado for decades. If Haley had at times suspected the hint of sadness in the judge's eyes when they rested on Isadora went beyond friendship, beyond regret, she never let on. Only after she'd turned to him to help her escape Frank Del Brio had she learned how much of a role he'd played in both her and her brother's life.

Carl Bridges hadn't been able to keep his old

friend Johnny from sliding into his brother Carmine's web, but he'd added his voice to Isadora's when she'd pleaded with Johnny to send Ricky off to a military school to keep him away from Carmine's thugs. The judge had also encouraged Haley to go up to Austin to attend his alma mater, the University of Texas, to keep her from discovering her father's growing entanglement with the Texas mob.

The ploy had worked. Until Haley spent two summers working in her father's office, she'd remained oblivious of the shady operations Carmine Mercado had dragged his brother into. Even after curiosity had led her to dig deeper into the family business than her job as a receptionist warranted, she'd pretended ignorance. She loved her father too much to confront him with the startling bits of information she'd picked up. She bled a bit inside whenever Johnny Mercado tried to bluster and disguise what he'd become from his family, but she kept his secrets tucked in a deep, dark corner of her heart. Now she'd take those secrets to the grave with her.

With a ragged sigh, she buried her doubts in the same watery grave. "You're right. I'm just... nervous now that it's really happening."

"We'll have to move fast," the judge warned. "I said I was going to drive around the lake and search for you. We'd better get you away before someone else decides to do the same. Stay here. I'll get the suitcase from the trunk.''

He was back before Haley could once more start to question what she was doing again. Mere moments later she'd changed into the outfit she'd bought and stashed with the judge in preparation for this night. The baggy tan slacks and loose-fitting top completely disguised her generous curves. Tucking her still-damp, shoulder-length hair up under a pixie-cut wig, she changed her brown eyes to a smoky green with tinted contacts. There wasn't much she could do about the little bump in her nose she'd inherited from her mother until she made a visit to a plastic surgeon, but the oversize glasses she slipped on would detract attention from it.

The judge was pacing the front room when she emerged. Running a critical eye over her, he nodded. "I hardly recognize you. Ready to go?"

She swallowed the bitter taste of guilt and regret. "Yes."

"Okay. Let's get you on your way."

Taking her elbow, he hustled her out to his car. "Your temporary ID, credit cards and passport are in the dash. I'll send new ones when...if you decide to go ahead with cosmetic surgery."

Gulping, Haley retrieved the documents and fingered the embossed passport. She could only guess the favors the crusty jurist had been forced to call in to manufacture her temporary identity.

"I'm sorry I pulled you into this mess, Judge."

"I've made plenty of mistakes in my life, missy. I don't count helping Isadora's daughter as one of them."

"I don't know how I'll ever repay you."

"I don't expect you to. Now duck down and stay out of sight until I get you to the rental I parked down the road earlier this afternoon. It's only a few miles."

The wily judge had thought of everything, even obtaining a nondescript sedan from a rental agency. Judge Bridges had made sure there was no way the car could be traced to him, or to the woman who'd park it at the San Antonio airport later tonight.

The drive to the hidden vehicle seemed to take forever, yet was all too brief. Haley crouched low in the seat, trying desperately to blank her mind to the frantic search she knew was taking place out on the lake. She'd made the wrenching decision to leave. For her father's sake, she had to follow through with it.

"Here we are."

Slowing, the judge pulled off onto a narrow track. Branches scraped against the sides of his car as it bumped down the path. When the headlights picked up the gleam of metal, he shoved the gearshift into park but left the engine running.

The hot Texas night wrapped around them as they made their way to the waiting Ford. Digging the keys out of his pocket, Carl passed them to Haley.

"You'll need some cash," he said gruffly. "Here's two thousand for immediate expenses. I'll wire more when you get settled."

"Judge, I—"

Her throat closed, tears burned behind her eyelids. This was it, the moment she'd both dreaded and planned for so meticulously. Her last seconds as Haley Mercado.

No, not as Haley Mercado. Haley was already dead. Lost beneath the dark waters of Lake Maria.

"You'd better get going," the judge said gruffly, his own voice thick. "It's a good stretch of road to San Antonio, and you have a plane to catch."

She couldn't get a single sound past the ache in her throat. Awkwardly, Carl patted her shoulder.

"Don't worry. I'll look after Isadora and Ricky. And I'll do what I can to extricate your father from the mess he's gotten himself into over the years. I can still pull a few strings 'round these parts."

Maybe then she could come home again. Clinging to that hope, Haley threw her arms around his neck and hugged him.

"I hope so, Judge. God, I hope so! Keep me posted, okay?"

"You know I will. Now scoot, girl, before we both start bawling like new-weaned calves."

She gave him another fierce hug, then slid into the sedan and waited while he backed his own car down the track. Its headlights stabbed into Haley's eyes. Almost blinded, she turned onto the paved road. She idled the car for a moment, waiting for the black spots to fade, then slowly accelerated. A few moments later a turn in the road took her away from Lake Maria.

In the weeks that followed, Carl Bridges was Haley's only contact with Texas and the life she'd left behind.

The judge's assurances that her family was working through their shock and grief sustained her through long days and lonely nights in strange cities. After a circuitous journey across several continents to cover her tracks, she found refuge in the comfy flat Carl had leased for her in London. There she found funds waiting to cover her expenses, including the cosmetic surgeon who altered Haley's features.

Under the surgeon's knife, her nose lost the little

bump she'd inherited from her mother, and her slanting, doelike eyes became rounded. She considered breast reduction and possibly liposuction to diminish her lush curves, but by then stress had carved off so many pounds that she carried a far more slender, if still subtly rounded, silhouette. Dying her hair a glowing honey-blond, she adopted a sleek, upswept style that gave her an unexpectedly sophisticated look.

With her degree in graphic arts, it didn't take her long to land a terrific job. She'd just begun to feel comfortable in her new skin when a call from Carl shattered her shaky sense of security. It came mere weeks after her supposed death. She could tell from his terse greeting that he was upset.

"What's the matter?" she asked, her pulse kicking into overdrive. "Are my parents okay? Ricky's not hurt, is he?"

"No, no one's hurt." His voice took on an odd note. "No one we know, anyway."

"Tell me, Judge. What's happened?"

"They found your body."

"What!"

"Some fishermen out on Lake Maria hooked on to a corpse. It's badly decomposed, but it matches your height and physical characteristics with uncanny exactness."

"Frank!" she breathed. "Frank must have planted it."

"That's what I'm thinking, too."

According to Carl, Del Brio had gone beserk when divers found his fiancée's halter top still tangled in the branches of the submerged tree. In a bitterly ironic twist, he'd insisted the local authorities arrest Luke and the others for taking Haley out on the lake and operating a high-powered speedboat while under the influence. Tests had confirmed a high level of alcohol in the men's blood, and now the four marines had been charged with reckless endangerment.

"All hell's broken loose 'round here," Carl related. "Your father wouldn't let Isadora view the corpse, but he and Ricky went down to the morgue. They both near about fell apart. Now even Ricky's out for blood. He's turned against Luke, blames him for taking you out in the boat when he was drunk."

"Luke wasn't drunk! I don't care what the tests showed. He was completely in control of himself that night."

"He's going to have to prove that in court. I don't know what kind of hold your uncle Carmine and Frank Del Brio have over the county D.A., but the idiot's upped the charges against Luke and the three others to manslaughter. They've been put on administrative leave from the marines and are being held in the county jail without bail until their trial.''

"Oh, no!" Shattered by the unforeseen consequences of her deception, Haley searched desperately for a way to clear the four men. "What about DNA tests? They'd prove the corpse isn't me."

"They would if we had a sample of your DNA to use for a comparison. Your mother's kept your room just as you left it, but she's had it thoroughly cleaned. We couldn't find so much as a hair caught in a comb or an old toothbrush to take a sample from.''

How like her mother. Isadora Mercado wouldn't allow a single mote of dust to settle on her precious daughter's belongings.

"I'll catch the next plane home, Judge."

"Now hold on a minute, missy."

"I won't let Luke and the others take the blame for my death!"

"Those boys aren't going to take the blame. I know more about the law than any six attorneys in this state, including that pea-brained D.A. I'll step off the bench to represent them and I'll get them off," he promised with utter confidence. "I'm only telling you about the fuss because I know you have the *Mission Creek Clarion* sent to a fake name at a post office box. I didn't want you to see the head-lines and have a spasm.''

"I'm pretty close to a spasm now!''

"Look, if it'll make you feel any better, go down to a newspaper kiosk tomorrow morning and buy a paper from Berlin or Hong Kong or anyplace but London. Take a picture of yourself holding up the paper and overnight it to me along with those before-and-after photos the plastic surgeon took of you. If worse comes to worst, I'll produce proof that you're still alive. I won't tell anyone where you are, though. You'll still be safe.''

"I will, but will you? If Frank finds out you helped me escape, he'll kill you.''

The judge huffed. "I'm an ornery Texan, missy, and tough as shoe leather. What's more, I've got a few tricks up my sleeve Frank Del Brio never thought of. You just send those pictures and don't worry about Luke and the boys.''

The sensational trial dragged on for months.

Haley followed its progress in the *Mission Creek Clarion*. The local paper remained sympathetic to the war heroes, but the Corpus Christi and Dallas dailies played up every scandal from the defen-dants' past.

Old feuds were resurrected, including the long-standing battle between Flynt Carson's great-grandfather and his former ranching partner, J. P. Wainwright. Tyler Murdoch's youthful brushes with the law after his mother abandoned him made for juicy copy. Spence Harrison's pre-law degree came into play as he assisted Carl Bridges in his own defense.

The tabloids may have had a field day with Flynt and Tyler and Spence, but they went for Luke's jugular. They seemed determined to paint him as rich and shamelessly indulged by the absentee uncle who'd acted as his guardian. Several papers ran disgusting, tell-all interviews with women Luke dated both before and after he'd joined the marines. Instead of a healthy young bachelor with normal appetites, he came across as an oversexed playboy who'd plied his best friend's sister with beer and coaxed her out on the lake so he and his buddies could take turns with her.

Despite the sensationalism, or maybe because of it, Judge Bridges made good on his promise to Haley. He got the four men acquitted.

The trial left its mark on all four defendants, though. They soon separated from the marines. Flynt took over management of the vast Carson ranching interests. Infuriated by the spurious charges brought against him, Spence went on to law school, spent his time in the trenches as a prosecutor, then campaigned for and won the D.A.'s job. Tyler disappeared into some shadowy, quasi-military organization. And Luke seemed determined to live up to the reputation as a playboy he'd gained during the trial.

Haley's heart pinched every time she read another story about the jet-setting millionaire. Invariably, he was photographed with some toothpick-thin supermodel or overendowed starlet hanging all over him. Once, she read that he was in London, attending the opening of a new musical he'd backed. She'd been tempted, so very tempted, to pay the outrageous sum the scalpers were asking for the sold-out performance to search the audience for a glimpse of Luke. But she didn't. She'd wreaked enough havoc on his life. She refused to take even the remotest chance that she might cause more.

That fierce resolve kept her in London for almost a decade.

Waves of homesickness attacked often during those years, especially at night. Determined to immerse herself in her new identity, Haley refused to give in to the despair that seeped into her heart whenever she thought of her family and friends.

Gradually the cosmopolitan city took her to its generous bosom. She grew to love the pigeons and the parks and the bright lights of Piccadilly Circus.

She even acclimated to the cold, foggy winters. Slowly she began to feel safe in her new identity. Carefully she built a small, intimate circle of friends.

She'd just returned from dinner with those friends when another call from Carl Bridges plunged her back into danger...and into Luke Callaghan's arms.

The call came on a muggy July evening. The phone was jangling in that distinctive European way when Haley unlocked the front door.

"Your mother's been beaten," the judge informed her with the closest thing to panic she'd ever heard from him. "Brutally beaten. The doctors..."

His voice wavered, cracked.

"The doctors aren't sure she's going to make it."

Haley caught a flight home that same night.

Four

The desperate need to reach her mother's bedside dominated Haley's every thought during the long flight from London to JFK, then on to Dallas and, finally, Corpus Christi. Exhausted but coiled tight as new barbed wire, she stepped off the jet to the rippling palms and ninety-nine percent humidity of the Texas Gulf. Too tense to even notice the sweltering heat, she rushed through the airport to the rental car desk.

Years of living under an assumed identity had honed her self-preservation instinct to a fine edge. Her altered features should give her anonymity, but just to be sure, she made a brief stop at a costume shop before leaving Corpus Christi. Improvising hastily, she explained that she'd been invited to a party that night, thrown by officers from the nearby naval air station. She left the shop with a nun's habit and wimple tucked under her arm. The convent of the Sisters of Good Hope was located just a few miles north of Mission Creek. Since the sisters made frequent visits to area hospitals, Haley would hide under their mantle until she determined just what the heck had happened to her mother.

The moist air of the coast followed her out of the city as she headed west on Highway 44. Soon the marshy flatlands of the coastal plains gave way to rolling hills cut by dry arroyos and dotted with mesquite, cacti and creosote. With the wind whipping her hair, Haley breathed in the hot, dusty air for almost an hour. At Freer, she turned left onto Highway 16 and headed home.

Home.

Her chest squeezed tighter with each familiar landmark. As much as she'd grown to love London's lights and glitter and sophisticated aura, Texas was home. In her heart, it would always be home.

She pulled off the road some miles north of Mission Creek to exchange her slacks and sleeveless turquoise silk sweater for the dove-gray habit. The long-sleeved dress raised an immediate sweat in the hundred-degree heat. Haley had to struggle with the wimple and short, shoulder-length veil, but finally got them right. The little makeup she'd had on when she'd answered Carl's call had long since worn off. Inability to sleep during the long flight had added a hint of grayness to her olive-hued skin. Satisfied that she more than looked the part, Haley slid back into the rental car and turned the air-conditioning up full-blast.

She kept her head averted when she passed Lake Maria. The memory of that awful night almost a decade ago still seared her soul. Mission Creek's historic downtown called her hungry gaze, however. The old granite courthouse looked exactly the same. So did the bank, founded in 1869 and still serving the local community. She flicked quick glances at Jocelyne's fancy French restaurant and the Tex-Mex favorite, Coyote Harry's. Her taste buds tingled at the remembered fire of Harry's Sunday special—huevos rancheros topped with mounds of French fries, all drenched in his award-winning chili. As hungry as she was, she had no thought of stopping. Her one goal, her one driving need, was to get to the Mission Creek hospital.

Luckily she arrived post-afternoon visiting hours and pre-supper. The staff was busy getting ready to feed the patients, and the visitors had all departed. Haley took the elevator to the second floor and picked the most harried candy-striper to ask directions.

"Excuse me."

The aide flicked her a quick glance. "Can I help you, Sister?"

"Yes, please. Which is Isadora Mercado's room?"

''Three-eighteen. Around the corner, at the end of the hall.''

''Thank you.''

Tucking her hands inside her loose sleeves in imitation of the nuns who'd taught her during her Catholic grade-school days, Haley glided around the corner. Halfway down a long corridor that smelled strongly of pine-scented antiseptic, she stumbled to a halt.

A heavyset man lolled in a chair at the far end of the hall, his nose buried in the paper. Haley guessed instantly he was one of the mob's goons. He had the disgruntled air of a man who'd rather be out shaking down pimps and two-bit dealers than spending empty hours in a hard, straight-backed chair.

What was he doing here? Why did Isadora need a guard? Swallowing a sudden lump in her throat, Haley lifted her chin and glided past the man. He gave her a curious glance and went back to his paper.

The door to Room 318 whispered open, then whooshed shut behind her. For a moment she thought she'd stepped into a hothouse. Glorious arrangements of gladioli, long-stemmed roses, and irises occupied every horizontal surface and filled the air with a heavy scent. Gaily colored balloons bobbed above the baskets. The room was such a riot of color that it took a moment for her to focus on the petite, slender woman hooked up to the bank of monitors beside the bed.

Despite Carl Bridges's warning that Isadora Mercado had been brutally beaten, the sight of one side of her mother's bruised, battered face had Haley reeling in shock.

"Oh, my God! What did they do to you?"

She couldn't hold back the soft, broken cry. In her horror, she forgot to color her voice with the light British accent she'd deliberately cultivated over the years. For that brief, paralyzing moment, she was Haley Mercado, ripped apart by anguish for her mother.

With agonizing slowness, Isadora's head turned. Bandages covered part of her face. What was exposed showed mottled bruises. Both eyes were swollen shut, but evidently the beating hadn't affected her hearing. Swiping her tongue along dry, cracked lips, she croaked out an agonized whisper.

"Haley? Is…is that you?"

Tears streamed down Haley's cheeks. She couldn't move, couldn't speak. She hadn't planned beyond this moment, hadn't formed a coherent strategy beyond just seeing her mother.

"Please," Isadora begged brokenly. "Please don't play this cruel game. Are you… Are you my daughter?"

Haley couldn't deny her mother's need, any more than she could deny her own. Sinking into the chair beside the hospital bed, she groped past the IV lines for her mother's hand.

"Yes, Mom. It's me."

A fierce joy lit Isadora's battered face. "I knew it! I knew all along you weren't dead."

Her fingers gripped Haley's convulsively. Tears squeezed through the swollen lids. Her throat worked, forcing out each hoarse, joyful word.

"Johnny kept insisting we had to accept the brutal truth. Even Ricky gave up and took out his grief on Luke and the others. But I never stopped believing you'd come home, Haley. Not for one minute!"

"Oh, Mom, I'm so sorry. So very, very sorry."

Overcome with guilt, Haley dropped her forehead onto their joined hands. For a moment the only sounds that filled the room were the soft beep of the IV pump and Isadora's quiet sobs.

As if seeking assurance, her mother reached across the bed with her other hand and patted her daughter's cheeks, her chin, her nose.

"What's happened to you? Your face, your bones. You feel so thin. So different."

"I've lost weight. And I had surgery, Mom. Just around the cheeks and eyes. And here. Feel my nose."

Her fingers trembling, Haley guided her mother's hand down the smooth, elegant slope the cosmetic surgeon had crafted.

"Our little bump is gone," Haley said, smiling through her tears. "I miss it. Almost as much as I've missed you and Daddy and Ricky."

"Oh, Haley!" Her bruised face contorting, Isadora gripped her daughter's hand with both of hers. "What happened that night, out on the lake? Where did you go? Where have you been all this time?"

She answered the easiest question first. "I've been in London."

"Why didn't you let us know you were all right?"

The anguish in her mother's voice cut her to the quick.

"I couldn't, Mom. I had to let you and Frank believe I was dead."

"Frank? Frank Del Brio is the reason you disappeared?"

"Yes."

"But you accepted his ring. You were engaged. I never understood why, but I thought…we all thought you must have seen something in the man the rest of us didn't."

"I did. His utter ruthlessness."

She debated how much to tell her mother. She

wasn't sure whether Isadora knew about her husband's involvement with the mob. Her parents had never talked finances or business affairs in front of their children. Haley herself would never have known about the shady side of the family business if curiosity hadn't made her dig deep during those two summers she'd worked in the offices of the Mercado Brothers Paving and Contracting.

As it turned out, Isadora was all too aware of her husband's involvement in his brother's schemes. Her fingers gripped Haley's brutally as she pinpointed the reason for her daughter's flight with uncanny accuracy.

"Frank threatened to expose your father, didn't he?"

Still, Haley hedged. She'd given up her family and the only home she'd ever known to protect her dad. It went hard against the grain to admit the truth, even now.

"Tell me, Haley."

"Yes, he did."

"I knew it had to be something like that. You wouldn't just disappear without good reason. Thank God you got away from that bastard. At least you're safe. Frank can't beat you to bring your father into line."

Haley reeled in shock for the second time in less than ten minutes. "Frank did this to you?"

"Oh, it was made to look like a mall parking lot mugging, but Frank was behind it. He wanted to let your father know he couldn't disobey orders from the family anymore."

No wonder one of Frank's goons sat outside the door. He was there to make sure Isadora Mercado didn't tell her story to the police. Resolve hardened inside Haley. Cold. Unwavering. Lethal.

"I'll see he pays for this. Whatever it takes, I'll see that he pays."

"Frank, or your father?"

The bitterness in her mother's voice shocked Haley into silence.

"Your father dragged us into this mess," Isadora said, baring her soul to her daughter for the first time. "You. Me. Ricky. All of us. I've been telling him for longer than I can remember that anyone who swims with barracudas will eventually get bloodied. Your father's in deep now, Haley. Too deep for you or Judge Bridges or anyone else to save him." Pain that had nothing to do with her bruises crossed her face. "So is Ricky."

"Oh, no! Ricky's working with Uncle Carmine?"

"I think so. He won't talk to me. He won't talk to anyone. He's turned so hard and distant since he broke off his friendship with Luke and Tyler and the others."

''This is all my fault. I should never have tried to get away by faking my death. I'll come home, Mom. I'll make things right.''

''No!'' Isadora's voice rose to a frightened croak. Clutching her daughter's fingers in agitation, she protested vehemently. ''No, you can't come home. I can't bear it if Carmine and Frank sink their claws into you like they have Johnny and Ricky. Please, Haley. Please go back to London. Today. Tonight. Let me know at least one of my family is safe and happy.''

Haley tried to calm her.

''I'll be careful, Mom. But I need to try to straighten out the mess my disappearance caused.''

''You can't. Don't you understand, it's too late for you to save your father. Too late for Ricky. Go back to London. Promise me you'll go back to London.''

In her heart Haley knew her mother was right. If she came home now, Frank would wreak a diabolic revenge for her attempt to escape him. Not just on Haley, but on her family. She was caught in a trap of her own making.

''All right,'' she promised, her throat aching. ''I'll go back to London.''

''Today?''

''Tomorrow. Today I'm going to spend as much time with you as I can.''

* * *

Mother and daughter said goodbye at nine-thirty that evening, with whispered promises to meet in Paris in the fall. It broke Haley's heart to leave Mission Creek without seeing her father or Ricky, but her mother had pleaded with her not to reveal herself to either. They were too close to Frank Del Brio and might let something slip.

She walked out of the hospital intending to make the drive back to Corpus Christi and catch a flight out in the morning, but the fact that she hadn't eaten since her dinner with friends back in London suddenly caught up with her. Hunger piled on top of her accumulated tension and jet lag to make her suddenly dizzy.

Food. She needed food before she tackled the drive back to Corpus. And something icy cold to drink. Coyote Harry's would be closed. So would the Mission Creek Café and pricey Jocelyne's. She didn't dare drive out to the Lone Star Country Club. She'd spent too many happy hours at the plush resort, counted too many of its patrons as her friends. After the pain of parting with her mother, she didn't need another reminder of all she'd given up when she'd left her home.

It would have to be the Saddlebag. The roadside bar was dark and smoky, but served the juiciest burgers this side of the Brazos. And since this was

Sunday night, the place wouldn't be as crowded as it was on other nights. With any luck, she wouldn't bump into anyone who'd known Haley Mercado.

She could hardly walk into a bar dressed as a nun, though. The disguise had allowed her to blend in at the hospital, but would make her stand out like a beacon in the Saddlebag. She'd have to trust in the cosmetic surgeon's skills and the new persona she'd perfected during her years in London.

With a quick look around to make sure the hospital parking lot was deserted, she pulled on her slacks and turquoise silk top and dragged off the wimple and hot, scratchy habit. Gulping in relief, she tucked a few loose honey-blond strands into the clip that held her hair up and added a touch of gloss to lips she'd chewed almost raw with worry.

Despite Haley's confidence in the person she'd become, every nerve in her body tingled when she pulled up at the weathered Saddlebag. The parking lot was nearly empty, thank goodness. So were the parking spaces of the ten or so motel units behind the saloon.

As she walked into the bar, she had to keep reminding herself that she was a different person now. Physically and emotionally. She hardly recognized herself when she looked in the mirror these days. Still, she half expected one of the patrons to shout her name and come charging around the long, curved bar to accost her.

No one shouted anything. Nor did Haley spot anyone she knew among the few patrons. The two women present gave her a curious once-over before turning back to their companions. The cowboys knocking balls around the pool table at the back of bar displayed considerably more interest in the newcomer, but Haley nipped it in the bud by simply ignoring them. Skirting the dance floor with a lone couple barely moving to a Trisha Yearwood ballad, she claimed a table in a dim corner.

"I'll have a cheeseburger," she told the waiter who appeared at her table a few moments later. "Medium well. And a lager. Draft."

"Lager, huh?" He cocked his head, studying her beneath the brim of his battered black Resistol. "You're not from around these parts, are you?"

Only then did Haley realize one of the British idioms she'd cultivated so deliberately over the years had slipped out.

"No, I'm not."

"Didn't think so. I'll bring your beer, uh, lager, right over to you."

"Thanks."

It wasn't the waiter who delivered the foaming mug some moments later, however. It was a tall, broad-shouldered cowboy with a silver belt buckle the size of a dinner plate and laughing blue eyes.

"This one's on me, beautiful."

Haley's heart stopped. Literally. She felt it thump, then contract, then simply die. She sat frozen, every nerve turning to ice as she stared at the strong, tanned face above the open collar of a crisp white shirt.

Her utter lack of response might have daunted a lesser man. Not this one. His mouth curving into a half grin, he deposited two mugs on the table.

"I figured if I brought one for each of us, I might just get lucky and be invited to join you."

She couldn't speak. She didn't dare. She prayed he'd take the hint and go away. Instead he seemed to regard her silence as a personal challenge. Not waiting for an invitation, he claimed the chair opposite hers.

"The waiter said you're not from around here. But when you first walked in, I could have sworn I knew you."

Her pulse kicked in with a painful surge. Panic raced along her iced-over nerves as his gaze lingered on her eyes, her nose, her carefully sculpted cheekbones.

"Have we met somewhere?" he probed, sprawling loose-limbed and comfortable in his chair. "Dallas, maybe? New York?"

She had to answer. She couldn't sit mute any longer. But it took everything she had to infuse her voice with polite disinterest.

"If we've met, I don't seem to recall it."

His grin widened at the deliberate put-down.

"Guess I'll have to see what I can do to make a more lasting impression this time."

Blue eyes gleaming, he tipped two fingers to the brim of his summer straw Stetson. "The name's Luke. Luke Callaghan."

Five

The blond stranger had drawn Luke across the bar like the scent of doe drew a stag. Not only was she gorgeous, but she'd appeared at the Saddlebag at just the right moment.

Luke had piled up almost three weeks of idle time since wrapping up a particularly nerve-bending covert operation deep inside a breakaway Russian republic. He was already bored with the free-wheeling playboy lifestyle he adopted between jobs for the shadowy government agency that had recruited him after he'd separated from the marines. He needed a distraction, and this delicious blonde certainly constituted that.

She'd hooked his interest the moment she walked into the Saddlebag. From a distance, she was stunning. Up close, she thoroughly intrigued him. Take the way she stared at him. Those huge brown eyes seemed to look right through him. Then there was the little hesitation before she returned his greeting. Her aristocratic nose quivered, and he could have sworn her hands trembled before she buried them in her lap.

If he made her nervous, she recovered quickly enough. Inclining her head in a regal nod, she acknowledged his introduction.

"How do you do, Mr. Callaghan?"

Luke had traveled extensively, both in the marines and in the dangerous operations that now took him to all parts of the globe. He placed her soft, lilting accent without difficulty. She was British. From London, probably, but she spoke with an odd inflection that he couldn't quite pin down.

"I answer better to Luke," he replied, waiting for her to reciprocate and offer her name. When she didn't, the decidedly male interest she'd piqued when she'd walked into the Saddlebag took on an added dimension. Now she stirred not only his masculinity. She challenged the rather unique skills he'd acquired over the past few years.

Only a handful of people knew about those skills. Or that Luke Callaghan now worked for an organization so secret its name would never appear on any governmental organizational chart. Luke hadn't told anyone in Mission Creek about being recruited by OP-12, even his four best buddies.

Three best buddies, he corrected with an inner grimace.

The thought of Ricky Mercado, who'd once

been closer than any brother, itched like a raw scab that refused to heal. Luke missed Ricky's friendship. He missed the good times they'd had, both at V.M.I. and in the Marine Corps. For that matter, he missed the corps. The old cliché was true. Once a marine, always a marine.

Unless you caused the death of an innocent young woman.

Then you had no business wearing the uniform of a United States Marine. No business holding yourself up as an example for your men to follow. Judge Bridges might have gotten his four defendants off, but Luke accepted full responsibility for the tragic accident. He should never have encouraged Haley to take the wheel. The speedboat was too big for an unskilled driver, its engines too powerful.

Despite the judge's warning to keep his mouth shut, Luke had freely admitted his criminal negligence during the trial. To this day he carried the guilt for that accident like a burr lodged just under his skin. He always would. It tugged at him now as he studied the stranger's face. She didn't look anything like Haley Mercado. Her face was thinner, the features were more defined. Yet for a moment there, when she'd first walked into the bar, Luke's pulse had hitched.

He tucked the memory of the young, vibrant

Haley into the corner of his heart where she'd always remain.

"Are you here in the States on business or pleasure?"

Her glance wavered, dropped to the beer she'd yet to taste. His went to the hands she wrapped around the frosted mug. No wedding ring, he noted. No rings of any kind. Short, oval-shaped nails polished the natural-looking shade women called French white for reasons Luke had never understood.

"Personal business," she said after a moment, meeting his gaze again. "But I'm just passing through Texas."

Well, well. Stretching out his long legs, Luke set out to seduce the woman across the table. It was a game he played, the same game all men played when they spotted a beautiful, unattached female. As often as not, he struck out. Occasionally he got lucky. In either case, he enjoyed the preliminary mating rituals that presaged getting to know a woman. Particularly a woman as delectable as this one.

"Too bad you can't spend more time 'round these parts."

"Why?"

"If you can get past the heat and the dust, this

corner of Texas isn't a bad place to sit and doterize awhile.''

The lazy drawl took some of the stiffness out of her spine. She sat back in her chair and rewarded him with the faintest glimmer of a smile.

'' 'Doterize'?''

''It's a local expression,'' he said with a grin that admitted he'd just made up the word up, ''for forgetting all your problems and pretty much doing nothing.''

''I see.''

She took a sip of her beer, leaving Luke more intrigued than ever. This cool, self-contained beauty certainly didn't suffer from an excess of volubility. Or curiosity. Most folks who'd just met someone for the first time would be launching a few discreet probes by this time. Either she wasn't interested or she was content to let Luke set the pace, which he was more than willing to do.

''So how do you occupy your time when you're not passing through Texas?''

She took her time before replying. Luke formed the distinct impression she was weighing what she'd tell him right down to the gram.

''I'm a graphic designer,'' she said finally.

''What do you design?''

Again she hesitated. The arrival of a platter of greasy fries and a cheeseburger provided an obvious excuse for her not to answer. With a murmur of thanks to the waiter, she squared the plate in front of her and arranged her face in a polite expression of dismissal.

"If you'll excuse me, Mr. Callaghan, I'm—"

"Luke."

"If you'll excuse me, Luke, I'm rather hungry."

No way was she going to shake loose of him that easy.

"Matter of fact," he replied, sniffing appreciatively, "so am I. Hey, Charlie!" He pointed to the burger slopping over the sides of her platter. "Bring another one of those, would you? Rare. And two more beers."

This was crazy! Absolutely insane! Behind Haley's polite mask, her thoughts spiraled perilously close to hysteria. She couldn't believe she was sitting across a table from Luke Callaghan, engaging in the seductive, sensual game played the world over by men and women who meet in bars.

She knew it was a game. She also knew that Luke was far more adept at it than she was. If the stories she'd read about him in the tabloids held even a photon of truth, the handsome, jet-setting millionaire had racked up more wins in this particular arena than any rock star or overmuscled, overpaid jock.

Common sense and the self-preservation skills Haley had honed these past years told her to push away from the table. Now. This very moment. Walk out of the smoky lounge. Walk away from Luke.

Maybe if the visit to her mother hadn't left her so raw and bleeding, she might have done just that. Or if she'd ever been able to exercise any common sense around Luke Callaghan. All the man had to do was smile at her in that careless way of his and she melted like the tangy cheddar dribbling over the sides of her burger.

She'd stay for another half hour, Haley swore silently. Just long enough to finish her meal. She wouldn't satisfy the curiosity that gleamed in his blue eyes. She couldn't. But she'd store up every minute of this unexpected interlude to take back to London with her.

She stuck to that plan through their burgers and beers. Luke downed his in man-size swallows. Haley took considerably smaller bites of the cheeseburger and nursed her second beer sparingly. She was fiddling with the mug, knowing it was time for her to leave, when another ballad drifted above the muted conversation and clack of pool balls. Martina McBride this time. One of her new hits that was just making its way across the Atlantic. A smooth, mellow song about an old love and missed chances.

Her gaze lifted to Luke's. An old love. Missed chances. A new life that had yet to bring her the private passion she'd once felt for this man. It was still there, she acknowledged. Buried deep under the layers she'd pulled over herself these past years, but still there. It would always be there.

"McBride's good," Luke commented, meeting her gaze. "Too good to pass up. Care to take a turn around the floor?"

A polite refusal formed on her lips. Luke saw it coming. In a preemptive move, he pushed back his chair, rounded the table and held out his hand. Memories of the disaster that had followed the last time she'd slipped her hand into his kept Haley in her seat.

"One turn." Undeterred by her obvious reluctance, he smiled. The tanned skin beside his eyes crinkled. "It'll help settle those fries."

Two seconds passed. Five.

Slowly, Haley entwined her fingers with his.

As she let him lead her to the dance floor, her doubts and insecurities fell away. One touch, and she knew this dance would lead to another. One feel of his body against hers, and she gave up fighting the hunger he stirred in her. Strangely she no longer felt the least hesitation. She wasn't a fright-

ened girl any longer, torn between her desire for
one man and the desperate need to escape another.
She was a woman, with a woman's needs and a
woman's cravings.

Tomorrow she'd honor her promise to her
mother and return to London. Tonight she'd create
an indelible memory to take with her.

Luke felt the change the instant he took her in
his arms. Without knowing how or why, he understood she'd altered the rules of the game. She
didn't put up so much as a token resistance when
he wrapped an arm around her waist and pulled
her against him. Thigh to thigh, they moved to the
music.

Lord, she felt good. As if she'd been molded to
fit to him. His chin grazed her temple, right where
curly strands feathered her forehead. Her high, full
breasts were positioned to cause the maximum dis-
ruption to his rational thought processes.

A corner of his mind warned that he knew next
to nothing about this mysterious stranger. Not even
her name. Yet her reticence didn't set off any silent
alarms. Not the kind that would have raised the
hairs on the back of his neck and made him check
the snubnose .38 he usually carried in an ankle
holster, anyway. Shutting down that busy, in-

tensely curious corner of his mind, he gave himself up to the pleasure of her body moving against his.

When the song ended, Luke didn't release her. She tipped her head back. Her brown eyes regarded him steadily. It wasn't a question he saw in their gold-flecked depths, but an invitation. Only too happy to oblige, he bent his head and brushed her lips with his.

If she hadn't already aroused him both mentally and physically, the taste of her would have done the trick. In a heartbeat he went from hard to aching.

His arm tightened around her waist. He considered inviting her out to his place, but she might bolt if he turned her loose long enough to make the twenty-minute drive. He was trying to figure out how best to get her out of the bar and into the closest bed when she answered the question he hadn't asked.

"Yes."

"Yes what?"

"Yes, I'll go to one of the rooms out back with you."

Whoa! Now this was getting lucky and then some! Disguising his astonishment behind a swift, slashing grin, Luke steered her back to the table. While she collected her clutch purse, he made a quick detour and tossed a fifty down on the bar.

"The key to the presidential suite, Charlie. And hurry."

"The presidential suite, huh?"

Grinning, the combination bartender/motel clerk slid a key across the smooth-grained oak. The unofficial designation of the largest unit was a joke among the several generations of cowboys who'd occupied it for varying lengths of times over the years, Luke and his friends included. From past experience, however, he knew it was clean, comfortable and recently renovated. He wouldn't take any woman there if it wasn't, much less this enigmatic, thoroughly arousing stranger.

As they crossed the parking lot, Luke half expected her to change her mind and call a halt to things. That she didn't surprised and aroused him all over again. By the time they reached the largest unit, he was walking with a hitch in his step.

He couldn't remember wanting a woman as much as he wanted this one. Maybe it was the secrets she held to herself. Or how she flicked her tongue along her lower lip in obvious nervousness. Yet she didn't so much as blink when he curled his hands around her upper arms and pulled her to him. He couldn't quite believe it when he heard himself offer her a last chance to back out.

"You sure about this, sweetheart? Not that I want to see you walk away, you understand. I'd just hate for you to wake up with regrets come morning.''

She made a small, choking sound. Sliding her palms up his shirtfront, she gave him a half smile. ''Oh, I'll wake up with plenty of regrets. But not about this. I'll never regret this.''

Luke would have had to be a hell of a lot more—or less!—of a man to hold back at that point. Swooping down, he captured her lip with his.

Her mouth opened under his. Warm. Willing. So incredibly erotic that the ache in his groin speared up, into his belly, and down, right to his boots. He'd had his share of women—more than his share, Tyler and Flynt and Spence often groused. He'd also developed one or two sophisticated techniques for finessing a woman out of her clothes over the years.

There wasn't anything sophisticated about the need that rose up now and kicked him square in the gut. Taking his cue from the way her fingers dug into his shoulders, he widened his stance, dragged her hard against him and drank his fill.

Or tried to.

The more he took, the more she gave, until Luke couldn't tell whose need kept them locked together, their bodies straining. All he knew was that he wanted this woman with a fire that burned clear through him. With a low growl, he fumbled the clip from the back of her head, thrust his fingers through the thick silk of her hair and anchored her head for his kiss.

All too soon, the mating of their mouths and tongues wasn't enough. For either of them. Bending, he scooped her up. They landed on the bed in a tangle of arms and legs and wild, searching hands. Shedding their clothes completely took more time and restraint than either of them possessed at that moment. Luke did manage to get her slacks and bikini pants down to her knees and her sweater off one arm. Gasping, she writhed under the skillful play of his hands and tongue and teeth on her breast.

He was full and heavy and pushing hard against his zipper when she went to work on his shirt buttons with frantic fingers. Suddenly she frowned. Panting and dewed with a fine sheen of perspiration, she fingered the raw, puckered scar in his left shoulder.

"What is this?"

"Just a scratch," he replied, swooping down to nip at her throat.

"Some scratch." She wiggled to one side and tried to get another angle on the wound. "Is that from a bullet?"

The last thing Luke cared about right now was

the souvenir he'd brought home from the break-away Russian republic.

"I dodged when I should have ducked," he admitted, raking his teeth lightly along the underside of her jaw.

"But what…? When…?"

He cut off the the questions he couldn't answer with a hard, hungry kiss. At the same time he hooked an ankle over hers and spread her legs. His hand slid down her belly.

Haley almost came apart when Luke slipped a finger inside her. He wasn't her first. She'd dated a good deal in college and indulged in a brief fling with a stockbroker in Dallas.

No man had ever claimed her heart, though. That had always belonged to Luke. And none had ever stirred such wild, white-hot sensations with his mere touch.

"Luke!" Gasping, she arched under his hand. The slow, deliberate strokes had her primed and poised on the edge. "I can't hold back much longer."

"Good," he growled, replacing his hand with the tip of his shaft. "Neither can I."

They made love most of the night. The first time was hard and fast and sweaty. The second, slower and sweeter, with Luke plying a cool washcloth over her body in ways she was sure were illegal in most South Texas counties.

The third was just before dawn, when he roused her from an exhausted doze and rolled her over, sleepy-eyed and protesting. She didn't protest for long.

The fourth came with the sun. She kept her eyes open this time, memorizing the curve of his shoulder. The short, wiry hair at the nape of his neck. The muscular slope of his back and buttocks.

When they finished, she barely had the strength to drag the spread over her sweat-sheened body and to aim a quick glance at the clock radio on the nightstand. It was late. Past eight. She'd have to hustle to get the car back to Corpus Christi and catch a flight to Dallas that would connect with the London direct.

"You want first dibs on the shower?"

"What?" Blinking, she dragged her gaze back to Luke.

"The shower. Do you want to hit it before I do?"

"It's all yours."

"There is another option, of course." Hooking a finger in the spread, he tugged it down an inch or two and dropped a kiss on her breast. "We could conserve water and soap each other down. I've still got a few washcloth tricks up my sleeve."

Haley summoned a smile. "Any more of your tricks and I won't be able to walk for a week. Better save them for next time."

He looked up then. His blue eyes narrowed. Behind the teasing gleam, they were keen and sharp. Too sharp.

"Will there be a next time?"

"Who knows?" Haley tossed back lightly.

She was gone when Luke came out of the shower.

He'd figured she would be. He hadn't missed the worried glance she'd aimed at the clock radio. Or the strained edginess to her smile.

He'd find her. He had the resources of a high-tech, covert agency at his disposal. When he did, he might just unlock a few of the mysterious stranger's secrets. That was his intent, anyway, until he drove home, logged onto his laptop and found a blinking light indicating a secure transmission from OP-12.

An hour later he climbed into the private, twin-engine jet he kept fueled and ready at the Mission Ridge airport and set a course for an isolated airstrip high in the Andes.

When he returned after six exhausting weeks, the beautiful stranger's trail had gone stone cold.

Six

Isadora Mercado died of heart failure three days after Haley returned to London. A devastated Carl Bridges delivered the news.

"She died peacefully," the judge related hoarsely. "In her sleep."

Shattered, Haley gave a small, animal moan and slumped against the wall behind her. His voice raw with his own pain, the judge tried to ease hers.

"I visited your mama the day she went. She was happier than I'd ever seen her. Knowing you were alive, that you were safe from Frank... It made all the difference to her, missy. Thank God you got to be with her when you did."

Still Haley couldn't speak. Her knees folded. She slid down the wall to the floor. Blindly she stared at the windows opposite her. A hard rain hit the panes, crying the tears that burned behind Haley's lids.

"Your father's made all the arrangements. She's going to be buried at St. Mary's, Haley. Beside you."

"Oh, Judge!"

"I know what you're thinking. You're thinking you should come home and be with your father and Ricky during their time of grief. Well, you can't. Your mother died with joy in her heart because she knew you were safe. You'll desecrate her memory if you put yourself right back in Frank's clutches."

Blinded by the tears that stung her eyes, Haley stared sightlessly at the window. She kept visualizing her mother's face as she'd last seen it, so bruised and battered.

"Mother told me she was convinced Frank was behind her beating. She was bitter at Daddy for still trying to straddle the fence. Playing Mr. Nice Guy even though his hands were dirty."

"He's always done that," Carl said in disgust.

"The trauma of that beating probably contributed to Mom's heart attack." Her fingers gripping the phone, Haley swore vengeance with a fervor that would have done her uncle Carmine proud. "Frank's going to pay for that beating. Someday he's going to pay!"

A month went by. Six weeks. London steamed in the July heat. August rolled in on waves of choking exhaust fumes. Services practically shut down as shopkeepers and government workers all took their annual holiday and jammed subways, trains and motorways.

Haley drifted through the jostling crowds. She took the tube to work, came home, avoided her friends. She felt as though she was living in a small, dark cocoon woven from grief, regret and bitter, corrosive anger. She couldn't seem to break the shell, couldn't find the energy to try. The heat drained her. Thoughts of her home and family haunted her.

All that saved her from complete despair was the memory of her stolen hours with Isadora.

And with Luke. The night Haley had spent in his arms would remain etched in her heart forever. She didn't realize how deeply until the first week in September, when the reason for her continuing lethargy finally sank in.

She was pregnant.

It took two trips to the pharmacy and three home-pregnancy kits before she could bring herself to accept the possibility. A visit to a women's clinic converted probability into fact.

She was pregnant.

Haley walked out of the clinic into bright September sunshine. Dazed, she made her way to the small park a few blocks from her flat. Pigeons fluttered and cooed from the statue of some forgotten general on his rearing charger. Leaves rustled in the oaks fringing the park. Bit by bit, the hard shell around Haley's heart cracked and fell away.

She was pregnant!

With a joyous whoop that earned her curious stares from passersby, she hugged her middle. She wouldn't be alone anymore. She wasn't cut off from her family any longer. She hadn't left Luke Callaghan behind forever.

She'd have his baby. Their baby. A new life to fill the void of her old. For the first time since Frank Del Brio had shoved that diamond on her finger, Haley's spirits soared high and free.

In her joy and eagerness, she welcomed the minor inconveniences and major physical changes that came with pregnancy. She also reestablished contacts with the small circle of friends she'd begun to make in London.

The days and weeks sped by. She spent hours converting the spare bedroom in her flat to a nursery. More hours with one of her married coworkers, shopping for the astonishing number of items a newborn evidently required. October brought gray skies. November, icy drizzle. December blew in cold and snowy, but Haley hardly noticed the weather. Happy and by now well-rounded, she thrilled at every twinge or kick that gave evidence of the life growing inside her.

January brought the first small indications that the nest she'd built for herself and her child might not be as safe and cozy as she thought. She let herself into her building, her cheeks rosy and her breath steaming from the cold, and noticed what looked like scratches around her mailbox lock. Frowning, she ran her gloved fingers over the faint marks. When she inquired of the doorman, however, he shrugged.

"Can't say how those scratches got there. Might a been workmen. We had a crew working in the lobby a few days ago. I'll check on it for you."

"Thanks."

When the doorman's inquiries returned no information about the marks, Haley shrugged them off, until a week later when she retrieved her mail and could have sworn that one of her letters had been opened. It was only a form letter, reminding her of her next dental appointment, but the joyous cloud she'd been floating on for months began to dissipate.

The hang-ups and wrong numbers began in late February, just weeks before her projected delivery date. The first two or three annoyed her. By the fourth or fifth, she had begun to feel distinctly nervous.

She didn't dare go to the police. She'd entered the country on a false passport, was living with forged identity papers. Nor could she contact her one rock. Carl Bridges didn't answer either his phone or the e-mails an increasingly worried Haley fired off. He'd told her he had some business to attend to and might be incommunicado for a while. But why did it have to be now? Just when she needed him.

In March, worry sent her into labor a week early, but she delivered a healthy, beautiful baby girl. She had her father's silky black curls and, Haley saw with a sob, his eyes. They were the color of a summer Texas sky. She named her Lena, after her mother's mother, Helena.

The next day she brought her baby home to the nursery she'd decorated so lovingly and prayed she'd be safe there.

Eight weeks later the taxi carrying Haley and Lena to the baby's two-month checkup took a wrong turn.

"This isn't the way," she informed the turbaned Sikh driver. "You should have turned right on Hyde Street, not left."

The driver stared straight ahead and whizzed down a broad street lined with leafless chestnut trees. Frowning, Haley leaned forward to rap on the Plexiglas partition separating the front seat from the back.

"Excuse me. You're heading in the wrong direction."

The driver didn't so much as blink.

Haley stared at the back of his head, ice forming in her veins. "Stop here," she ordered. "Let us out."

In reply, he flicked a switch. All four door locks clicked down.

Panic raced through Haley, swift and all-consuming. She wasn't afraid for herself, but for her baby. Dear God, her baby!

Snatching Lena from the carryall, she cradled the newborn against her chest. A dozen frantic schemes jumped into her mind. She'd roll the windows down at the next traffic stop. Scream for help. Pass Lena out the window to a pedestrian. Tell him or her to run like hell.

She never got the opportunity to implement any of her wild schemes. Mere moments later the cab swerved onto a side street. Halfway down the block, a blue painted garage door rumbled up. The cab slowed, swerved again and rattled into the garage. The blue door dropped down with a clank.

After the bright sunshine outside, the gloom of the windowless garage was impenetrable. Haley clutched Lena to her shoulder, almost frantic with fear for her child. Suddenly dazzling white light flooded the garage. She couldn't see a thing, but she could hear.

The door locks clicked.

The driver climbed out and opened the rear passenger door.

Footsteps sounded on concrete.

Blinking furiously to clear her vision, Haley made out two figures approaching the cab. One she didn't recognize. The other had her gasping.

"Judge!"

Giddy with relief, she started to scramble out of the cab. The jurist's haggard expression halted her. He looked defeated, utterly, completely defeated. His shoulders slumped. His white hair lay lank and disordered, as though he hadn't combed it in days. Behind his black-framed glasses, his faded blue eyes held pain.

Belatedly, it occurred to Haley that Frank might have had the judge kidnapped. Maybe he'd been tortured. Or fed drugs. Forced to disclose his role in the supposed death of Haley Mercado. She shrank back against the seat, Lena clutched to her shoulder.

"It's okay, Haley." Desolation wreathed the judge's face as he coaxed her from the vehicle. "Please. Come out. We have to talk to you."

She emerged slowly, warily. Her glance darted to the man beside Carl. Short and stocky, with hair a bright shade of copper, he wore a nondescript gray suit and a bulldog expression.

Behind him, three others moved out of the gloom, watching her with dark, intent eyes.

"Who are these people?" she asked the judge, her heart pumping hard and fast.

"This is Sean Collins. He's a special agent from the New York office of the FBI."

Oh, no! All Haley could think of at that moment was that the FBI had busted Carl for procuring her fake passport and identity papers. Depositing the sleeping Lena in the carryall still resting on the back seat, she whirled and launched into a passionate defense.

"Judge Bridges isn't the one to blame for any wrongdoing. He was acting as my agent when he obtained that forged passport. I'm the one responsible. I had to get out of Texas, out of the States."

"We're not here to talk to you about a forged passport," the agent identified as Sean Collins replied.

"Then why are you here?"

"Because we have reason to believe your mother didn't die of natural causes."

Shocked and confused, Haley turned to the judge. "What's he talking about? You told me Mom had a heart attack."

"She did," Collins answered for him. "But

based on evidence only recently uncovered, we obtained a court order to have her body exhumed. The medical examiner performed an autopsy and discovered traces of potassium chloride in her body. We think someone slipped the drug into her IV and deliberately caused her heart to fail.''

"Frank," Haley whispered hoarsely. "Frank must have done it to keep her from talking."

"Actually," Collins explained, "our guess is that Del Brio killed her because she wouldn't talk. Word is, he was hot to know the identity of the nun who visited her right before her death. He's been asking a lot of questions about the Sisters of Good Hope. Questions that led us to theorize Isadora's daughter might still be alive."

Pain splintered through Haley, cutting into her heart like a thousand needle-pointed shards. Her face now as haggard as the judge's, she stared at the agent through a haze of despair.

"I killed her. My visit. That disguise. I killed my mother."

"No, you didn't!" Snapping out of his near stupor, Carl grasped her arm. "You listen to me, missy. Your visit filled your mama with profound peace. Knowing you'd escaped made up for what she'd had to endure all these years."

"But—"

"No buts!" he said fiercely. "Isadora and I

talked for years about taking you kids and leaving
Mission Creek. She never forgave Johnny for dragging all of you into the morass with him. But he
was her husband, and you and Ricky needed your
father and—''

''And she was a devout Catholic,'' Haley finished for him. ''She didn't believe in divorce.''

Nodding, he let out a ragged sigh. ''God knows,
I tried my damnedest to talk her into one. I loved
her, Haley. I've loved her for as long as I can remember.''

''I know, Judge.''

She sank back against the taxi fender, her
thoughts whirling. Shock and pain gradually sharpened into fear. If Frank Del Brio had grown so
suspicious that he was trying to track the nun
who'd visited Isadora, he could be closing in on
her. That would explain the scratches on her mailbox and sudden spate of hang-ups.

Nausea rolled around in Haley's stomach. As
sickening as it was, she had to face the truth. She
couldn't run far enough to escape Frank Del Brio.
As long as she lived—as long as he lived—she'd
never be safe.

Nor would Lena.

Agent Collins apparently agreed. ''We're only a
few steps ahead of Del Brio, Miss Mercado. We're
just lucky that we were able to convince Judge

Bridges to tell us what he knew of Isadora Mercado's mysterious visitor. He brought us to you because he now realizes the life you've so carefully constructed for yourself in London is about to come tumbling down around your ears. We need to get you and your baby away from here and to provide you both with protection.''

"In exchange for what?'' Haley asked, wary of strangers bearing gifts.

"We'll talk about that later.''

"No, we'll talk about it now. I want to know exactly what you want from me, Mr. Collins.''

Palming his thick reddish hair, the agent chose his words carefully. "The FBI has been building a case against your uncle Carmine for years. After his health had begun to fail and Frank Del Brio moved up to number two in your uncle's organization, we've shifted a lot of our attention and our assets to him. We thought we had him nailed awhile back on extortion and racketeering charges, but the bastard eliminated both of our key witnesses.''

"So how do I make up for the loss of those witnesses?''

His hazel eyes drilled into hers. "We need someone inside, Miss Mercado. Someone who understands the power structure. Someone who wants to take down Frank Del Brio as much as we do.''

The enormity of what he was asking of her left Haley speechless. Collins used her stunned silence to press home his point.

"You worked at Mercado Brothers Paving and Contracting for two summers, Miss Mercado. You know the family business. Enough of it to understand what looks right and what doesn't, anyway. We're hoping you can help us ferret out times, dates, drop-off points, contacts. Anything that will tie Del Brio to the smuggling and racketeering operations we know he runs."

Haley cleared her throat. "Let me make sure I understand you," she said carefully. "You want me to infiltrate the mob. Spy on Frank Del Brio. Gather evidence against him. And by the way, gather evidence against my father and possibly my brother, as well."

"We're prepared to offer you a deal. Immunity for your father and brother in exchange for the detailed information we need to indict Del Brio. We'll also place your baby with a family who'll love and protect her while you're undercover."

"No!" she said fiercely. "No deal! I'm not giving up my baby. She's only two months old."

"I understand how you feel," Collins replied gravely. "I know you'd do anything to protect her. Anything."

"You bastard! You're deliberately playing on my fears for my baby to gain my cooperation."

"Maybe. But you've got plenty to fear, Miss Mercado."

She hated him in that moment. He was only voicing the brutal truth she'd already admitted to herself, yet Haley wasn't prepared to hear it said out loud. Nor was she prepared to give up her baby, even temporarily.

"I have to think. I need some space. And some time."

"I'm afraid time is the one thing you don't have much of, Miss Mercado. We'll give you what we can, though. We've already booked a room for you in a hotel under an assumed name. We'll take you there."

Another assumed name, Haley thought on a wave of near hysteria. Another carefully constructed identity. More background details to memorize. More lies to dish out. She'd already told so many she wasn't really sure who she was anymore.

True to his word, Agent Collins gave Haley space to think. Time ran out all too swiftly, however.

Collins showed up at her hotel room the very next afternoon. Judge Bridges was there, still worn, still haggard. The judge took one look at the agent's face and moved to stand behind the sofa where Haley sat cuddling Lena.

"What's wrong?" she asked, already afraid of the answer.

"Someone broke into your flat last night, Miss Mercado. Scotland Yard managed to lift some good prints. Evidently the perp was one of Del Brio's henchmen. If we're going to get you out of London and into a new identity, we'll have to move quickly."

This was the way it would always be, Haley thought with an ache in her chest. Constantly running. Always looking over her shoulder. Worrying every time she dropped her daughter off at day care or nursery school. Unless and until the threat to Lena was removed.

Closing her eyes, she kissed her baby's black, downy curls. She had no choice. She had to help Collins destroy Frank Del Brio and dismantle the operation her uncle had built. But she was damned if she'd place her baby with strangers.

There was only one person she'd trust with Lena. One man who possessed both the power and the resources to protect her. Only one other person with a parent's responsibility.

"All right," she told Agent Collins. "I'll go back to Texas with you. I'll work undercover. But

I won't place Lena in the care of strangers. I want her to go to her father."

"That can be arranged."

The judge eyed her curiously. He'd respected Haley's privacy when she'd declined to identify Lena's father and said merely that she intended to raise her child on her own. Now she she had no choice when he voiced the question she saw on his face.

"Who is the father, Haley?"

"Luke. Luke Callaghan.

Seven

Ten days later Haley stared intently into a lighted makeup mirror. She and a small army of FBI agents had been holed up in a motel in Clearwater Springs, twenty miles east of Mission Creek, for more than a week now, perfecting her cover and orchestrating her transition to her new identity.

The transition was now complete. Another stranger stared back at her from the lighted mirror. Frowning, she forked her fingers through what she could only call her mane, now permed and dyed a lighter blond.

"Fluff it up more than that," the female agent observing her directed. "We're going for real Texas-style big hair here."

"I was born and lived most of my life in Texas," Haley said with a wry smile. "I never wore my hair this big."

"You do now," the FBI specialist replied, returning her assortment of combs and brushes to a gray steel case. "Don't forget, the intent is to exaggerate, exaggerate, exaggerate. Draw the eye from those features we didn't have time to alter to those we did. Now pouf those curls out another inch or so.''

Grimacing, Haley complied, then studied the result in the mirror. She had to admit the makeup artist knew her business. The slender Londoner who'd lived in Haley Mercado's skin for so many years had disappeared. In her place stood Daisy Parker.

A loose tumble of butterscotch curls framed her face. Botoxin injections had added a ripe, sensual fullness to her lips. Her eyebrows were now thicker, darker. Purple shadow and the liberal application of mascara and liner gave her eyes a sultry air. A short black skirt and a blouse unbuttoned to display a hint of cleavage completed the transition. The look stopped short of barroom cheap, but definitely came down on the other side of refined.

It would do, she thought grimly. It would have to do.

Besides, the only person she really had to fool was Luke Callaghan. The cosmetic surgery she'd undergone in London had altered her enough that she'd be a stranger to everyone except him. Hopefully, he wouldn't match this gum-snapper with the sophisticate who'd flamed in his arms.

An impatient rap rattled the bedroom door. "Are you finished in there? It's almost six-thirty."

"We're finished," the agent called. Closing her steel case, she gave Haley a warm smile. "Good luck, Miss Mercado. Sorry. I mean, Miss Parker."

The two women emerged into a small sitting room still curtained against the night. Dawn was beginning to break, though. Faint fingers of pink showed at the edges of the blinds. This was it. The first day of her new life as Daisy Parker.

Taking in a deep breath, she faced the team of FBI operatives who'd assembled to craft and train this new entity. Communications technicians. Documentation specialists. Evidence-gathering experts. The language coach who'd spent hours coaxing Haley to grossly exaggerate her native Texas drawl and smother the faint British lilt she'd so carefully cultivated.

Planting his hands on his hips, their team leader ran a critical eye over his creation. "Good," Sean Collins murmured in approval. "Very good. You'll fit right in with the other waitresses at the Lone Star Country Club."

"If I get the job."

"You'll get it. Don't forget, Daisy Parker has waited tables at some of the best clubs and restaurants in Dallas and Fort Worth. If the manager checks your references, he'll get nothing but glowing reports from your former employers. Just don't drop too many trays your first day or two.''

''I'll try not to.''

The bald-headed language coach wagged an admonishing finger. ''Tut, tut! Let's have that again, shall we?''

With a sardonic glance in his direction, Haley laid it on with a trowel. ''Ah'll surely to goodness try not to drop anythang, cowboy.''

''Excellent,'' the coach beamed. ''Excellent.''

Special Agent Collins checked his watch. ''All right, folks. This is it. Operation Lone Star is officially under way. You ready, Judge?''

All eyes turned to Carl Bridges. He glanced down at the baby tucked into the combination baby carrier/car seat by his side and nodded. ''I'm ready.''

''Wait!''

Haley rushed across the room. She'd kissed and cuddled Lena for hours last night. The good-natured baby had cooed happily, waving her fat, dimpled fists and blowing bubbles from her rosebud mouth until she'd dropped into sleep. This morning Haley had barely gotten her diapered, changed and fed before the FBI makeup artist arrived with her box of magic tricks.

Now that the moment of separation had arrived, Haley had to hold Lena again, had to kiss her soft curls and breathe in her powdery scent one last time. Collins had warned Haley that this undercover operation could take months. The thought of missing all those weeks of her baby's development drove a stake right through her heart.

Folding back the baby's fluffy pink blanket, she tucked the well-fed, sleepy child against her. Doubts about the elaborate scheme Carl Bridges had worked out to deliver Lena to her father without revealing the identity of her mother had her throwing an anxious look at the judge.

"You're sure Luke will be at the country club this morning?"

Understanding her reluctance to part with her baby, Carl Bridges nodded and went over the same ground they'd already covered half a dozen times.

"Luke, Flynt Carson, Tyler Murdoch and Spence Harrison have a standing six-fifteen tee time every Sunday morning. Depending on how crowded the course is, they generally finish the first nine holes around eight."

"Yes, but—"

"I called Luke last night on the pretext of wanting to invite him to lunch at the club. He suggested brunch instead, after he and the others finish their round. He'll be there, Haley."

"Daisy," Collins corrected from across the

room. "We all have to start thinking of her as Daisy."

"Daisy," the judge echoed. "Don't worry, missy. I won't put Lena on the ninth tee box until I see Luke and the others holing out on number eight."

"You're sure they won't be able to see you?"

"I'll be in the groundskeeper's shed. It's separated from the tee box by a thick hedge. I found a spot where I can slip Lena's carrier through the hedge, watch the guys approach, then skedaddle."

"What about the note? Do you think we got the wording right?"

Patiently, he quoted from memory the phrases the entire FBI team had helped draft and redraft.

Luke—
I'm your baby girl. My name is Lena. Please take good care of me until my mommy can come back for me.

Nuzzling her baby's downy curls, Haley fought a wave of fierce, last-minute doubts. "I hope we're doing the right thing!"

"I hope we are, too," Sean Collins muttered.

He'd argued against leaving Lena with Luke, who lived right there in Mission Creek. He'd wanted to place her with a couple in Nebraska so

Haley wouldn't catch glimpses of her child and become distracted. "Out of sight, out of mind" was his strategy.

She'd pointed out that she'd worry far more about Lena if she couldn't see her occasionally and know she was being well cared for. Collins had caved finally, with the caveat that the note indicate that Lena's mother had departed the area. The last thing he wanted was for folks to connect the baby found on the ninth tee with the new waitress at the Lone Star Country Club.

"It's getting late," the judge warned. "I'd better take her, Haley."

"Daisy!" Collins snapped. "Haley Mercado is dead. From now on we all think and talk Daisy Parker, even in our sleep!"

"Duly noted," the judge retorted, a half a breath away from cutting the FBI agent down to size. "Here, let me have her, Daisy."

Haley swore she wouldn't cry. She hadn't cried since the day her mother died. She didn't have any tears left to shed. But her throat felt as though she'd swallowed a bucket of broken glass when she dropped a feather-light kiss on her daughter's crown and passed her to Carl.

She couldn't know that was the last time she'd hold her child for more than twelve terrifying months.

Eight

Present day

Now, over a year later, Haley stood in the shadows of the Saddlebag's noisy bar and wondered how it all could have gone so wrong.

She'd done exactly what Sean Collins had asked. She'd spent more than a year undercover. She'd gathered more than enough evidence for the FBI to take down Frank Del Brio and destroy his network. She'd dodged and sidestepped and somehow managed to keep from tangling herself in the web of lies she'd lived with daily.

In that time her uncle Carmine had died. Carl Bridges had been murdered. And Frank had managed to strip away Daisy Parker's layers one by one. The bastard had not only escaped the net the FBI had tried to throw over him, he'd kidnapped her baby.

Now her cover was blown. Operation Lone Star was falling apart. And Luke Callaghan had yet to hold his child in his arms.

That wasn't entirely her fault, Haley reminded herself with an ache just under her ribs. Carl Bridges had placed Lena right where the four Sunday morning golfers would find her. Who could have anticipated that water from the sprinkler-wet hedge would drip onto the note and obliterate the father's name? Or that Luke wouldn't show that morning, of all mornings?

He'd been gone for months. Long, angonizing months, while Haley watched from a distance as Flynt and Josie Carson cared for Lena. Endless, torturous months, when she lived every hour of every day on the edge. And then, when Luke finally returned to Mission Creek, he was blind in both eyes.

Her heart aching, Haley stared across the smoke-filled bar at the man she'd been in love with for as long as she could remember. His back was to her, but she recognized the short, curly black hair showing under his straw Stetson. Recognized, too, the strong column of his neck and the athletic shoulders under the denim shirt. She should. She'd run her hands and mouth over those strong, muscled shoulders repeatedly the night they'd created their child. The child she'd do anything—anything!—to get back safely.

Dragging in a ragged breath, she threaded a path though the tables. The man sitting opposite Luke saw her first. Tyler Murdoch's brown eyes narrowed as he tracked her approach. He lounged in a comfortable slouch, his chair tilted back against the scarred paneling. The lazy sprawl didn't fool Haley. Nor did she fail to note how he kept his back to the wall. Evidently his recent marriage to a fiery Spanish interpreter hadn't dulled the mercenary's razor-edged instincts.

"Look's like we've got company, buddy. It's Daisy Parker, the waitress from the country club."

She caught Murdoch's murmur. Caught, too, the way Luke's head cocked to one side. Just an inch. Maybe two. Like a cougar listening to the rustle of the dry Texas grass. Or a stallion scenting danger on the wind.

Her heart hammering, Haley stopped beside his chair. The stress of the past months showed on his face. Beneath the rim of his hat, she could just make out the trace of white scars from the shrapnel that had blinded him. Could see, as well, the deep grooves bracketing his mouth.

Despite the scars, despite the strain carved into his face, Luke Callaghan was still the most elemental male Haley had ever encountered. His startlingly blue eyes might not register anything except darkness now, but they stared straight ahead with disconcerting directness. And his mouth. Lord, his mouth! Haley could almost feel it on hers again as she drew her tongue nervously across her lower lip. Shedding her poured-on Texas twang like last year's winter coat, she murmured a soft, urgent request.

"I need to talk to you, Luke. Privately. Please!"

Luke recognized her voice.

He'd always heard that people who'd lost their sight honed their other senses to a razor's edge. If so, these past six months had proved him the exception to the general rule. Neither his sense of smell nor his tactile abilities had sharpened to any appreciable degree since the explosion deep in the jungles of Central America that had left him totally blind, until this last week when he'd begun to see dark shadows. He wouldn't have said that his hearing had improved all that much, either, but this woman's voice was burned into his memory.

He'd heard it before right here at the Saddlebag. Two years ago. She'd spoken with more of British lilt then. Not with Daisy Parker's thick, down-on-the-border accent, nor the subtle one he heard now. The suspicions about the waitress Luke had been harboring for some weeks now hardened into certainty.

"I want to talk to you, too," he ground out in a tone so low and dangerous she took an involuntary step back.

He heard the small shuffle. The sudden, nervous movement had him shoving back his chair. Following the sound, he reached out. His hand closed around her upper arm, but not before his knuckles made contact with a full, lush breast.

His entire body went taut at the touch. Memories of that night two years ago knifed into him. She'd welcomed him so eagerly that night, so generously. As though she'd been waiting for him all her life. When he'd come out of the shower the next morning, though, she'd disappeared.

Luke had made a few inquiries about her. After the mission that had taken him high into the Andes, he'd exercised some of his special contacts within the government in an attempt to locate the gorgeous blonde. He'd finally concluded the lady had had her reasons for slipping away with the dawn. Only recently had he begun to connect the beautiful stranger with the waitress who'd started work at the Lone Star Country Club right about the time his buddies discovered a baby on the ninth tee.

His baby. The child he'd never seen. The child who'd been kidnapped right before his return to Mission Creek. The child, he was now certain, this cold-hearted witch had callously abandoned.

"We'll talk outside," he growled.

Behind him, Tyler called a quiet question. "Need me to come along, buddy?"

"No. This is between Daisy and me."

The brutal grip on her arm told Haley this confrontation was going to be even tougher than she'd anticipated. Luke held her manacled, as though he didn't trust her not to bolt. He also, she noted in the small corner of her mind that wasn't numb with fear for her child, threaded his way through the tables with an assurance that gave no hint of his impaired sight. He let her guide him, following her lead with a sure tread, but to a casual observer they must have looked like any couple slipping away from the noisy bar to one of the motel units out back.

Deliberately, Haley blanked her mind to the night when they, too, had done just that. This wasn't about her and Luke, or about that night. This was about Lena. Only about Lena.

After the air-conditioned smoke of the bar, the humid June night wrapped around them like a sponge. Haley didn't mind the heat or the humidity or the dust that swirled on the night air. After all those years living in London's damp, misty climate, she and Lena had come home to wide-open skies and the blazing Texas sun. She could only pray that they'd never have to leave again.

"My car's parked near the back of the lot," she told Luke.

"Lead the way."

The beat-up sedan the Bureau had supplied her with when she'd first gone undercover looked like a small, stray dog amid the herd of muscled SUVs and pickups. The white van that had followed her from the safe house was still parked a few rows from the rust-spotted sedan. Haley didn't see the agents who'd driven it, but suspected they weren't far away. After all, she was the FBI's best hope— their only hope!—for luring Frank Del Brio out of hiding.

She reached for the handle of the passenger door, thinking Luke would slide into the seat so they could talk inside the vehicle, but he used his grip on her arm to swing her around. The sedan's roof was to her back. A large and obviously angry Luke crowded close at her front. Too close.

Planting his hands against the car, he caged her. The brim of his Stetson shadowed his face, but she couldn't miss the muscle that ticked in the side of his jaw as he fought for control.

"You're her, aren't you?"

"Her?" she murmured, stalling for time while she tried to figure out where to begin her tangled explanations.

The question seemed to add to the anger that radiated from Luke in waves. The muscle at the side of his jaw jumped again.

"Don't mess with me, lady."

Haley had known him all her life. She'd also spent the most passionate night of her life in his arms. Yet this was a Luke Callaghan she'd never seen. Hard. Cold. Dangerous. He might have thoroughly intimidated her if she hadn't lived with fear so long that she'd learned to tip her chin and stare it straight in the eye.

"You're the woman I hooked up with here at the Saddlebag two years ago." It wasn't a question this time, but a flat statement. "You weren't passing yourself off as Daisy Parker then, but it was you."

"Yes, it was."

His breath hissed out. For a moment, maybe two, that night hovered between them. Haley ached to reach up, to touch his cheek. To beg him to fold her into his arms again and to let her lose herself in his heat and strength. Suspecting what was to come, she kept her fists clenched tightly at her sides.

"We made more than love that night, didn't we? We made a baby."

"Yes," she whispered again.

"So you brought our daughter back to Mission Creek. Thought you'd cash in on her, big time."

"Cash in on her?" Shocked, she gaped up at him. "What in God's name are you talking about?"

He leaned closer, crowding her against the car. "I'm guessing you came back intending to initiate a nice fat paternity suit. But her millionaire father was gone. Out of the country. Unreachable. So you dumped the kid on the golf course at the country club, where some other rich sucker was sure to find her, and walked away."

"No! That's not how it happened!"

"That's exactly how it happened. Flynt Carson told me he and Tyler and the others found the baby in a carrier, with only a blurred note that gave her name. Christ, how could you abandon your own child like that?"

"I didn't abandon her! You don't understand—"

"You're right, I don't." Scorn laced every word. "I don't understand how any mother could leave her child in the care of total strangers. But I'm getting the picture now. I'm also beginning to understand why Lena was supposedly 'kidnapped' from Flynt Carson's ranch."

"Supposedly?" Her voice spiraled to a near screech. "There's no 'supposedly' about it!"

"Come on, sweetheart. You don't have to play-act anymore. You dumped the kid because no one knew where I was and you got desperate. You could have waited until I came back to Mission Creek to establish paternity. The DNA results would have made that a breeze. But you hit on a better scheme, didn't you? Instead of child support spread out over a number of years, you decided on a nice, fat ransom paid all up front. You won't get it,'' he warned in a voice so cold it could have cut glass. ''You won't get a cent from me that way.''

''Oh, God!'' Stunned, she tried to wrap her mind around his accusations. ''You think I arranged to have my own child kidnapped so I could extort money from you?''

His lip curled. ''Prove me wrong, Daisy. Tell me you didn't come to the Saddlebag tonight to deliver a ransom demand.''

''Luke, listen to me. You've got this all backward.''

''How much?'' he snarled. ''Tell me, dammit! What's the asking price for a baby these days?''

''All right! They want two million!''

''Two million, huh?''

Luke would have paid ten. An hour ago he would have cashed in every stock and bond he owned to buy the safe return of his child.

He didn't understand this urgent need to hold this daughter he'd never seen. He wanted a family, sure. Someday. He'd spent most of his childhood in boarding schools under the loose guardianship of his uncle, but Stew had shown far more interest in the leggy showgirls he wined and dined in Vegas than in his nephew.

The military had become Luke's substitute family. First at V.M.I., then in the marines. Although he'd shed his uniform after being charged with contributing to Haley Mercado's death, the tight bonds forged during his years in the service had provided all the kith and kin he'd needed. Until he'd learned he had a daughter.

Tyler Murdoch had delivered the news. Deep in a steamy jungle, right after the explosion that had sent shards of shrapnel slicing into Luke's face.

The knowledge that he'd fathered a child had sustained Luke throughout the painful operations that followed. He'd come home to Mission Creek blind but determined to do right by his daughter. Determined, too, to find the woman who'd abandoned her. He'd pictured her frightened. Desperate. Unable to care for her baby and driven to the extreme of leaving her on a golf course. He could have forgiven her that.

What Luke couldn't forgive was that the baby had been kidnapped just days before his return to Mission Creek. The timing was too close to write off as mere coincidence. More to the point, the evidence he'd so painstakingly gathered over the past months implicated this waitress in Lena's disappearance.

Disgust bit into him, so deep and bitter he could taste it. He still didn't know who she really was or where she'd sprung from, but he was sure of one thing. When they recovered Lena—which they would—there was no way in hell Luke would leave his daughter with this sorry excuse for a mother.

Bringing his face down to within inches of hers, he stripped matters to their core. "Let's get one thing absolutely straight between us, lady. You're not getting one cent from me, let alone two million. But you are going to take me to wherever you've stashed our baby. We'll sort matters out from there."

Haley snapped. After all she'd been through, after all the stress and false identities and lies she'd been forced to live, Luke Callaghan had the nerve, the unmitigated, unfettered, unqualified gall, to accuse her of using her own baby in a scheme to extort money from him! With a surge of fury, she shoved at his chest and opened enough space between them to spit out her rage.

"Listen and listen good, cowboy! You're dead wrong on every count but one. The man who snatched our child has demanded a ransom, but I didn't come here intending to shake you down for the two million. I don't want your money, Callaghan!"

"Is that right?"

"That's right, dammit!"

He looked anything but convinced. "Then what do you want?"

"Your help. You're the one man I can take with me when I go after my baby."

"Right." Skepticism cut deep into his voice. "Because you've suddenly decided to admit I'm her father?"

"No, you jackass. Because you're blind."

He reared back, jerking away as if she'd hauled off and open-handed him. He recovered almost immediately, though. She'd give him that. Whatever else Luke had lost in the jungles of Central America, he could still spring to the attack with lethal agility.

"Why don't you run that by me one more time?" he suggested with biting derision. "I'm having a little trouble understanding exactly how my impaired vision plays in this situation."

"I'll tell you exactly how it plays. I just got a call from the kidnapper. He told me to get together two million in unmarked, nonsequential bills. He said he'd contact me later with instructions on when and where to deliver it. At the same time, he swore... He warned..."

She choked. Swallowing hard, she forced out the words that sliced at her throat like shards of glass.

"He warned that I'd never see Lena alive again if there was a police officer or a federal agent anywhere within a hundred miles when I make the delivery. That's why I'm asking—why I'm begging you to go with me. He'd suspect anyone else, think I was trying to set him up, but he wouldn't... That is, he couldn't..."

"He wouldn't worry about a blind man."

She bit her lip, hating to throw his disability in his face but determined to use whatever weapon she could.

"Look, all I need is for you to distract Frank, to divert his attention for a few seconds. I'll take it from there."

"Frank?" His black brows came together. "Are you talking about Frank Del Brio?"

"Yes. We suspected it all along. After the shootout the other night, we were certain. But until he called a little while ago, we didn't know what he wanted for her."

Luke reached for her again, his hands fumbling until they locked around her upper arms. He pulled her up, as if to feel and not just hear what she had to say.

"Who's 'we'?" he demanded fiercely. "Who the hell are you, Daisy? And what's your connection to the Texas mob?"

She hesitated, trying to decide which bomb to

drop first, searching for a way to lay bare the secrets she'd buried deep inside her for so long.

Suddenly the slamming of car doors ricocheted through the night, followed by the thud of running footsteps. The sound triggered an instant response in Luke. Shoving Haley behind him, he spun to meet the threat he could hear but not see. Pinned against the car, she wiggled frantically until she made out the shadowy figures rushing toward them with weapons drawn.

"Move away from her!" the lead runner shouted.

She felt Luke tense, sensed him readying to spring.

"It's okay!" Grabbing the sleeve of his blue denim shirt, she held him back. "They're FBI!"

"What?"

The two agents fanned out to either side, weapons held high, no doubt remembering Sean Collins's terse instructions to keep his star witness safe at all costs.

"Move away from her, Callaghan. Slow and easy. Keep those hands right where we can see them."

Luke complied. He took a step to the side, his hands held at waist level.

Breathing out a sigh of relief, Haley shoved her hair out of her eyes and eased out from behind the protective shield of his body. The lead agent kept Luke covered while he speared her with a quick glance.

"You okay, Miss Mercado?"

The man beside her went still. Absolutely still.

"Mercado?" he echoed softly. Dangerously. "Did he just call you Miss Mercado?"

Nine

Haley swallowed a curse. She'd imagined a hundred different scenarios in which she finally revealed her real identity to Luke. None of those scenarios had been played out in a parking lot, with guns drawn.

Nor had she expected this sudden, Arctic silence. Disbelief, yes. Anger, of course. The kind of deep, visceral anger a man once accused of causing Haley Mercado's death was entitled to feel. She suspected that would come, though, and soon.

Delaying the inevitable, she answered the agent's question first. "Mr. Callaghan wasn't threatening me. We were just talking."

"Didn't look much like talking from where we sat," he returned. "You sure you're okay?"

"Yes."

He eyed Luke speculatively. "Want us to hang loose while you finish your chat, Miss Mercado?"

"No. Please, just leave us alone."

"All right. If you say so. But we're close if you need us."

They retreated to the van, shutting the doors behind them. Stillness settled over the parking lot once more. The hot, dusty quiet plucked at Haley's raw nerves like a hag with boney fingers. Bracing her shoulders, she turned to Luke.

He might have been carved from the granite dug out of the hills of north Texas. He stood rigid, unmoving, his eyes narrowed to slits. As if he could actually see her. As if he was trying to strip away the layers of lies and deceit with which she'd cloaked herself.

"I wanted to tell you the truth, Luke. You and the others. I couldn't."

He didn't answer. The silence stretched tight and thin. He broke it with a savage command.

"Get in the car."

"What?"

His jaw worked. "Get in the car. You've got some serious explaining to do, Miss Mercado. I've got a few things to say to you, too, but I'll be damned if I'll say them in a parking lot with the FBI and God knows who else listening in."

The white van followed them all the way to Luke's sprawling estate on Lake Maria.

Since the Callaghans had made their millions in oil and the stock market, the property Luke had inherited didn't run to thousands of acres like the

GET 2 BOOKS FREE!

To get your 2 free books, affix this peel-off sticker to the reply card and mail it today!

MIRA® Books,
The Brightest
Stars in Fiction,
presents

Superb collector's editions of the very best books by some of today's best-known authors!

★ **FREE BOOKS!** To introduce you to "The Best of the Best" we'll send you 2 books ABSOLUTELY FREE!

★ **FREE GIFT!** Get an exciting surprise gift FREE!

★ **BEST BOOKS!** "The Best of the Best" brings you the best books by some of today's most popular authors!

GET 2

HOW TO GET YOUR
2 FREE BOOKS AND FREE GIFT

1. Peel off the MIRA® sticker on the front cover. Place it in the space provided at right. This automatically entitles you to receive two free books and an exciting surprise gift.

2. Send back this card and you'll get 2 "The Best of the Best™" books. These books have a combined cover price of $11.98 or more in the U.S. and $13.98 or more in Canada, but they are yours to keep absolutely FREE!

3. There's no catch. You're under no obligation to buy anything. We charge nothing – ZERO – for your first shipment. And you don't have to make a minimum number of purchases – not even one!

4. We call this line "The Best of the Best" because each month you'll receive the best books by some of today's most popular authors. These authors show up time and time again on all the major bestseller lists and their books sell out as soon as they hit the stores. You'll like the convenience of getting them delivered to your home at our special discount prices . . . and you'll love your *Heart to Heart* subscriber newsletter featuring author news, horoscopes, recipes, book reviews and much more!

5. We hope that after receiving your free books you'll want to remain a subscriber. But the choice is yours – to continue or cancel, anytime at all! So why not take us up on our invitation, with no risk of any kind. You'll be glad you did!

6. And remember…we'll send you a surprise gift ABSOLUTELY FREE just for giving THE BEST OF THE BEST a try.

BOOKS FREE!

THE BEST OF THE BEST™ — Here's How it Works:

Accepting your 2 free books and gift places you under no obligation to buy anything. You may keep the books and gift and return the shipping statement marked "cancel." If you do not cancel, about a month later we will send you 4 additional books and bill you just $4.74 each in the U.S., or $5.24 each in Canada, plus 25¢ shipping & handling per book and applicable taxes if any.* That's the complete price and — compared to cover prices starting from $5.99 each in the U.S. and $6.99 each in Canada — it's quite a bargain! You may cancel at any time, but if you choose to continue, every month we'll send you 4 more books, which you may either purchase at the discount price or return to us and cancel your subscription.
*Terms and prices subject to change without notice. Sales tax applicable in N.Y. Canadian residents will be charged applicable provincial taxes and GST. Credit or Debit balances in a customer's account(s) may be offset by any other outstanding balance owed by or to the customer.

cattle ranches owned by the Carsons and Wainwrights, Mission Creek's two most prominent families. The house sat on five hundred acres of prime real estate, though, bounded by the lake to the east and low, rolling hills to the west.

Haley pulled up at massive wrought-iron gates, which slid open at a click of the thin, quarter-size remote dangling from the key ring Luke dug out of his pocket. When she drove through, the gates slid shut again.

"Stop here for a moment," Luke snapped.

Aiming the remote at some invisible target, he clicked out a code. Haley neither saw nor heard any evidence of the security system he was obviously reactivating, but she guessed it would be elaborate given his long and frequent absences from Mission Creek.

While her rust-spotted sedan idled just inside the gates, the FBI van rolled to a halt outside. Its headlights blazed in her rearview mirror. She half expected the driver to lean on the horn and demand entrance, but he must have radioed the FBI command center for instructions. A moment later the van backed up and parked beside the stone gatepost.

Seeing the FBI settling in on the other side of the gate raised an odd, prickly sensation on Haley's skin. She'd worked with them for more than a year, passing information, receiving coded instructions. Now Sean Collins's team was on the other side of the fence, literally, and she was on her own.

No, not on her own. She was with Luke.

The prickly sensation intensified, raising goose bumps all up and down her arms.

"It's set," the man beside her said tersely. "Just follow the drive. The house is about a mile up."

"I know."

Her soft reply didn't go down well. Like Haley, Luke had to be remembering the little sister who'd tagged along when Ricky had come to shoot pool or to check out the lasted foal sired by the Callaghan championship stud. The same little sister Luke had believed dead all these years.

"That's right," he bit out. "You do."

He stared straight ahead into his own private darkness while Haley negotiated the drive. The tires swooshed on the tarmac. A smooth, manicured lawn rolled down to the lake. A shiver rippled along her spine as she glanced off to the left. She couldn't see the water in the darkness, but she knew it was there.

She had so much to explain, so much to account for. Dreading the ordeal ahead, she brought the car to a stop under a tall portico supported by white columns on either side. A massive wrought-iron coach lamp hung suspended by chains, illuminating the wide front steps and double doors framed by additional lamps. Easing out from behind the wheel, Haley rounded the front of the car to take Luke's arm.

"I've learned to count the steps," he informed her, shaking loose of her hold. "I manage in my own home."

"Sorry."

"Just walk ahead of me."

He wasn't just counting his steps, she realized a moment later. He was listening to the echo of her footfalls, first on the drive, then on the stairs, and pacing himself accordingly. Once he'd gained the wide porch, he moved with confidence.

Skimming his left hand down the door, he found the key slot and inserted a narrow plastic card with his right. The card unlocked the door and activated the lights inside. Brushing past him into the soaring, two-story foyer, Haley waited while he reinserted the card, this time into a wall unit that contained several rows of infrared discs and a palm-size screen.

"That's a pretty elaborate security system," she murmured.

"Tyler designed it to my specifications. The sensors emit silent pulses instead of sound." His mouth twisted. "The sequencing of those pulses allows even a person who can't see to pinpoint the location of an intruder without letting him know he's being tracked.''

Like a panther stalking its prey in the night.

With a little shiver, Haley followed him into the living room just off the hall. The cavernous room faced east, with a long wall of windows to let in the morning light. The windows were shuttered now, and the only illumination came from a desk lamp that flickered on at their approach. The inch-thick Persian area rugs that used to cover the oak floorboards had been removed, she saw. Probably so Luke wouldn't trip over them. The floor plants were gone, too, no doubt for the same reason.

The man-size sorrel-leather sofas and chairs were still there, though, arranged in comfortable groupings facing the massive stone fireplace that dominated the room. So was the rack of the Texas longhorns mounted above the mantel. A good twelve feet long, the horns speared to sharp tips.

Haley's glance drifted to the exquisitely woven Mexican blanket draped across the back of one sofa. The colorful throw was a treasured gift, she knew, from the couple who'd acted more like surrogate parents to Luke than his own, irresponsible uncle.

''I hope we didn't disturb Mr. and Mrs. Chavez, coming in so late like this.''

''They moved out of the main house into the

guest cottage three years ago,'' Luke informed her in a clipped tone. ''They needed space for their grandkids to romp and tear around when they come to visit.''

With four bedrooms, a wraparound porch, and a breathtaking view of the lake, the guest cottage was larger than most family homes. The Chavezes' lively brood would certainly have room to romp. The rest of the staff, Haley remembered, lived off the grounds. So it was just her and Luke, all alone in this two-story mansion.

As if reading her thoughts, he tossed his hat onto one of the chairs, hitched his hips against a high sofa back and folded his arms. ''All right, Haley. No one's going to interrupt us now. You've got a few things to explain. Why don't you start with your miraculous resurrection from the dead?''

She ran her tongue over dry lips. She'd held her secrets for so long, guarded every word, measured every lie, that she had to drag the truth from deep inside her.

''I'll have to begin before my resurrection.''

''Begin wherever the hell you want,'' he said with brutal callousness. ''Just get on with it.''

Haley shoved her hands into the front pockets of her jeans. It shamed her to admit she'd run away. Shamed her even more to admit the reasons why.

"I don't know how much you knew about my family's business," she began.

"I'd heard rumors," Luke said acidly.

More than rumors. Hell, he couldn't have formed such a close friendship with Ricky and not suspected the source of the Mercado family income.

"Then you have some idea of the kinds of things my uncle Carmine was involved in. He and Frank Del Brio."

"Oh, I've got a good idea what your fiancé was involved in."

Stung by the derision in his voice, Haley fired back. "I didn't get engaged to him by choice, you know."

"No, I don't know. If you didn't want to marry Del Brio, why the hell did you wear his ring?"

"Because Frank knew every detail of my father's involvement in Uncle Carmine's operations. He threatened to leak what he knew if I didn't marry him."

"I only met your uncle a couple of times," Luke scoffed, "but I can't see Carmine Mercado allowing anyone to set up his brother and force his niece into marriage against her will."

"Can't you? Maybe that's because you're an outsider. You don't understand the family. My uncle wanted me to marry Frank. Carmine trusted him. More than he trusted my father by that time. So I went along with the engagement. I had to. But I began plotting my escape the same day.''

''Right. Your escape.'' His jaw hardened. The disdain in his voice took on the cutting edge of disgust. ''You don't have to tell me about your escape. I was there, remember? So were Tyler and Spence and Flynt.''

His fury flared white-hot. Leaping across the room, it singed Haley from head to toe.

''Do you know how many frantic hours we spent searching for you? Do you have any idea of the guilt we've all carried since that night?''

''Yes, I—''

''No, lady, you don't. You can't. Any more than you can imagine how it feels to stand trial for the wrongful death of your best friend's sister.''

''I didn't mean for you to take the blame! Any of you! I intended to slip away during the barbecue that night. I'd planned to leave my sandals and coverup by the shore so people would think I'd gone swimming and drowned. But when I went out in the speedboat with you and we almost hit that tree, I—I took advantage of the situation.''

''You sure did. Just out of curiosity, whose decomposed body did they pull out of the lake?''

''I don't know. I'm guessing Frank arranged to have that body dropped in the lake to solidify the case against you. He would have wanted you and the others to pay for his fiancée's supposed death.''

Luke gave a short, bitter laugh. ''That's understating the case considerably. Del Brio did everything but bribe the jury. Hell, for all I know, he probably did that, too.''

''Carl said he tried.''

''Carl? Carl Bridges?''

''Yes.''

''Let me get this straight. You were in communication with my attorney?''

''Yes.''

''During the trial?''

''Before, during and after,'' she admitted. ''The judge helped me slip out of the country. He arranged for a fake passport and got me set up in London. He was also the one who told me about the trial. I know you won't believe me, Luke, but I wouldn't have let you or the others take the blame. I was ready to jump a plane and come home as soon as I heard charges had been filed against you.''

''Sure you were.''

''The judge talked me out of it. He swore he'd get you off. I sent proof that I was still alive, just in case, but he never had to use it.''

''So why did you come back?'' he demanded.

''That night, two years ago, when I bumped into

you at the Saddlebag, why did you come out of hiding then?''

''I came back to see my mother. She was in the hospital. She'd been badly beaten. It was made to look like a mall mugging, but it was a warning to my father to tow the line.''

That pulled Luke up short. With a low, savage oath, he pictured the woman who'd always treated him with the loving warmth she showed her own son.

''I'd heard Isadora was hospitalized, but after the trial things got so bad between me and your family that I didn't want to upset her with a visit. She died soon after that, didn't she?''

''Yes, she did.''

She couldn't have feigned the raw pain in her reply. A good chunk of Luke's anger melted as the enormity of what she was telling him sank in.

''I need a drink,'' he muttered. ''How about you? I keep some cognac here in the bar, but I could brew coffee or—''

''Cognac's fine.''

Measuring his steps, he crossed to the built-in bar and felt for the Waterford decanter glinting in the soft light. The heavy crystal stopper chinked as he removed it and nudged brandy snifters under the decanter's lip. After pouring healthy portions for both of them, he carried the snifters back across the room and held one out.

When Haley reached for it, her fingers brushed his. The heat was still there, Luke discovered with a jolt. The same glowing spark they'd fanned into flames two years ago.

Retreating, he moved to the sofa. Haley followed his lead. Luke heard the soft whoosh of the leather cushions as she settled in a chair on the far side of the marble slab that served as a coffee table.

"So you came home to visit your mother," he said, picking up where they'd left off. "After which you stopped in at the Saddlebag for a drink and we ended up in bed."

"Yes."

He heard the wince in her voice at his phrasing, followed by a blunt honesty that surprised him.

"Just for the record, I don't regret that night, Luke. I could never regret it. It gave me Lena."

The anger he'd tried to bank came back, swift and fierce. "Funny. For a moment there, you sounded as though you almost regret abandoning our child."

"I didn't abandon her!"

The fragile crystal sang out as Haley snapped it down onto the coffee table.

"I couldn't keep Lena with me while I was undercover."

That caught Luke's attention. In the past hour he'd come up with a dozen different reasons in his mind for Haley to be posing as a waitress at the Lone Star Country Club. The possibility that she might be acting as a federal agent wasn't one of them.

"I've been working with the FBI for over a year now," she revealed, "helping them build a case against Frank."

Well, that explained the guys who'd jumped them in the parking lot. Frowning, Luke tried to sort through the details of her incredible story.

"I don't understand. You engineered your own death. You lived in London for years under an assumed identity. You'd just had a baby. Why did you suddenly decide to go to work for the feds?"

"The FBI said they had evidence my mother didn't die of natural causes. Someone injected potassium chloride into her IV."

Luke shot upright, splashing cognac onto his hand. "The hell you say!"

"The FBI thinks she was killed because she wouldn't disclose the identity of the stranger who…who visited her in the hospital."

The small, anguished quaver wasn't lost on Luke. He stored it away to think about later, when he had time to sort through his thoughts. Right now it was all he could do to absorb the tale she went on to tell of tampered mail and phone hang-ups.

"I realized I'd never be safe as long as Del Brio was free," she finished. "More to the point, I knew Lena would never be safe. That's why I decided to cooperate with the FBI. First, though, I had to make sure Lena was cared for while I was undercover."

"So you left her on the golf course?" he asked incredulously. "That's your idea of ensuring she was cared for?"

"She was left where her father would find her. Only you were gone that particular Sunday." Her tone took on an edge of sharp accusation. "You stayed gone for months. Dammit, where were you when your daughter needed you?"

Not particularly happy at being put on the defensive all of a sudden, Luke fired back. "One, I didn't know I had a daughter. Two, I didn't know she needed me. Three— Oh, hell. Three doesn't matter. All that matters now is Lena."

Haley could have wept with relief. After all the hurt and anger and guilt, they agreed on the only point that mattered. Her hands clutched tight, she waited while Luke downed the rest of his cognac with a distinct lack of respect for its age.

"All right," he said grimly. "The past is past. Let's cut to tonight. I want to know exactly how

Del Brio contacted you. Exactly what he said, word for word. Any background noises or sounds you might have picked up. Any significant nuances in his voice.''

An hour later Haley was limp with exhaustion. She hadn't slept more than a few hours since the shoot-out three nights ago. Frantic fear for Lena and worry over her father had wrung her inside out. Luke's relentless grilling sapped the small reserve she had left.

"That's it," she said hoarsely after she'd repeated every detail for the fourth time. "That's how Frank left it. He'll let me know when and where to deliver the ransom."

"We have to assume he'll know how to reach you. He tracked you to the FBI safe house. He'll track you here. I'll contact Sheriff Wainwright and…"

"No!"

Haley's sharp protest earned her a swift frown.

"Frank said not to let Justin or the FBI in on the ransom delivery," she reiterated. "That's why I came to you, Luke. I can't…I won't risk Lena's life in another shoot-out."

He conceded with a curt nod.

"All right. But we'll need help to pull this off. I'll get Spence and Tyler over to rig some electronics on the phone lines. Flynt can go to the bank for me tomorrow and retrieve the two million. In the meantime...''

''In the meantime?''

''You'd better get some rest. You sound as if you're about to drop.''

''I'm okay.''

''You can't help your daughter if you're too exhausted to think straight,'' he said with brutal candor. ''Stretch out on the couch here if you don't want to go upstairs, but for God's sake get some sleep.''

She couldn't have climbed that wide, curving staircase if she'd wanted to.

''All right. I'll take the couch. Do you mind if I use the phone first to call the hospital? I want to check on my father.''

''Of course I don't mind,'' he said, then added gruffly, ''he was holding his own when I called ICU this afternoon.''

''You checked on my dad?''

''Your parents were good to me, Haley. After you died—disappeared—I couldn't bridge the gap that opened between us, but I still cared about them. Go ahead, make your call. I'll wait in the den and make mine when you're finished.''

He was almost out of the room before Haley worked up the courage to call to him.

"Luke."

He half turned, angling his head in that careful, listening way. "Yes?"

"Thank you."

"For what?"

"For listening. For putting the past behind you. Most of all, for helping me with Lena."

His face hardened. "She's my daughter. Whatever I can do for her, I will. We'll work out the arrangements for her future when we get her back."

As he made his careful way down the hall, Haley felt the blood drain from her face. Good Lord! Did Luke intend to battle her for custody? Could he use the fact that she'd had to place her baby in safekeeping against her? Would she wrest Lena away from Frank only to lose her to her father? The prospect tightened the band of fear around her heart.

She couldn't handle another crisis right now, Haley decided bleakly. She'd just check on her father, then curl into a tight ball here on the sofa, close her eyes and picture her baby's happy face.

Ten

Luke stood in the den he'd converted to a clean, utilitarian office and tried to rein in his chaotic thoughts. He still couldn't quite believe the woman down the hall was Haley Mercado. Sweet, curvaceous Haley Mercado.

He'd known her since grade school, for crissake! He'd watched her transition from coltish girl to precocious teen. By the time he and Ricky and the others returned from the Gulf War, Haley had blossomed into full, sensual womanhood. Luke might have seriously reconsidered his self-imposed hands-off policy at that point, but muscle-bound Frank Del Brio had beat him to the punch. He'd claimed Haley as his and, assuming any of the incredible story she'd just strung out was true, had driven her to incredibly desperate measures to escape him.

Was the story she'd just fed him true?

Despite his anger, his instincts said yes. He'd spent enough time with Ricky to sense how closely Johnny Mercado flirted with danger. Luke could well believe he'd gotten himself in so deep that Del Brio had plenty to coerce Haley with. Looking back, he could almost—almost!—understand her crazy reasoning for deciding to disappear.

Damn! For more than a decade she'd pretended to be dead, only to then risk everything by going undercover for the FBI. His first call would be to the Bureau, he decided grimly. He'd sure as hell get verification before he—

A small sound cut into his whirling thoughts. Every one of his senses went on instant alert. He stood still, listening intently.

The muffled noise came from the living room. Trailing his fingers along the wall, Luke moved silently down the hall.

She was crying. Quietly. Agonizingly. From the sound of it, she'd buried her face in cushions, but nothing could completely drown the wrenching sobs.

Luke stood just beyond the arch, his jaw working. This woman had played him for a world-class fool. Repeatedly. First by letting him and his friends take the fall for her death. Then by pretending she was a stranger that night at the Saddlebag. Not to mention failing to inform him about the small matter of their child. Luke sure as hell wasn't going to let her twist him inside out again.

Gritting his teeth, he started back for the office. He took two steps. Three. Stopped.

The utter desolation in those muffled sobs ripped at him. Swearing viciously, he swung around again. A moment later he gathered her into his arms.

Startled, she tried to jerk away. "Wh-what are you doing?"

"Damned if I know."

Holding her loosely, he eased them onto the sofa. The leather whooshed under his weight, the cushions tilting so that Haley rolled against him. Gulping, she tried to halt the wrenching sobs.

"I'm sorry. I didn't mean to— I don't—"

"Shhh." Cupping the back of her head, he cradled her face in the hollow of his shoulder. "It's okay."

"No, it's not." Blinking furiously, Haley dragged in a hiccuping breath. "I feel like an idiot. I never cry."

Not since her mother's death, anyway. She'd shed all the tears she had in her then. Tonight, though, her emotions were stripped to the bone.

"We'll get her back," Luke said gruffly, zeroing in on the cause of her distress with pinpoint accuracy.

She wanted desperately to believe him, but the brutal reality of the situation made a mockery of hope. "You don't know Del Brio like I do. He'll stop at nothing to get what he wants. Nothing!"

"Del Brio doesn't know me, either. Whatever it takes, we'll get Lena back."

The flat certainty in his voice tilted her head back. Blinking away the teary residue clinging to her lashes, she studied the face so close to hers. Luke stared straight ahead, his blue eyes unblinking but fierce. Stubble shadowed his cheeks and chin and made the white scars on his temple stand out in stark relief.

The evidence of his pain distracted her momentarily from her all-consuming fear for her baby. Oh, God, what had really happened in that jungle in Central America? How much had Luke suffered? Her fingers trembling, she lifted a hand to trace the spidery scars.

Luke sensed the movement and abruptly brought his head around to meet it. In the process, his lips grazed her palm.

They both went still, each waiting for the other to pull away. His mouth was hot and damp under her palm. Her skin burned where he touched it. Seconds ticked by with agonizing slowness, each one seeming to take months and then years with it, until Haley was at the Saddlebag again, aching for this man with all the passion she'd kept bottled up inside her for so long.

No, not this man. She hadn't really known the Luke Callaghan she'd given herself to that night, any more than he'd known her. With all their secrets, they were strangers then. They were strangers now.

It took everything Luke had to pull away. He didn't trust this woman, and sure as hell couldn't trust the desire that knotted his belly and almost made him forget who she was. Still, he couldn't bring himself to release her. Not yet. Not while her tears still dampened his neck and tension held her in a tight coil.

"You've got to let it go and get some rest, Haley."

"I wish I could," she murmured, her breath a ragged sigh against his neck.

"Blank your mind for a few moments. Just wipe away every thought."

"I can't."

"Yes, you can," he countered, recalling the technique that had saved his sanity during his weeks as a POW. "Don't think. Don't feel. Don't paint any pictures in your mind. Just imagine a blank canvas. A big, white, empty space."

She tried too hard. Her lashes feathering his neck, she scrunched her eyes shut. He felt her tension and frustration as she searched for the emptiness.

"Relax, Haley." He lowered his voice to a slow, hypnotic murmur and began to stroke her hair. "Just relax. Wrap yourself in a haze. A soft, gray haze."

"Like a London fog."

"Like a London fog, only warmer. It covers everything. Smooths all the jagged edges. Dulls the sharpest fears. Feel how soft it is? How warm it is?"

She gave a little grunt, wanting to be convinced but not quite there yet. Luke continued the unhurried stroke, smoothing her hair, calming her with his touch the way he'd calm a skittish colt.

"Let the haze surround you. Drift through you. There's nothing there. Nothing but a cloud of cotton."

Silence dropped over them. Moments went by. Slowly, so slowly, she slipped into that half state between worry and mindlessness. Luke felt her muscles slacken, then a little jerk as she resisted dropping into sleep.

"It's okay, Haley. Let yourself go. You're warm and safe and secure."

He murmured the words without thinking. Not until she gave a little moan and curled against him did he realize how desperately she must have craved both security and safety all these years.

With a silent curse, Luke set out to lull her back

to sleep. Planting his boots on the polished marble coffee table, he eased down until his head hit the sofa back and did his damndest to ignore the press of full, rounded breasts against his chest.

Haley drifted awake to the scent of fresh-brewed coffee. She let the aroma tease her groggy senses for long moments before prying her eyes open. They felt dry and scratchy, the way eyes always did after a bout of tears.

After all the years and months of hiding her every thought and emotion, she couldn't believe she'd dissolved into such a pitiful bundle of incoherence last night. Or that she'd fallen asleep in Luke's arms.

At a loss to explain either his actions or her own, she tossed back the blanket and swung her stockinged feet to the floor. A quick glance at the cheap watch she'd worn in her Daisy Parker persona showed it was just past 5:00 a.m.

Panic darted through her at the thought that she might have slept through another call from Del Brio, but logic quickly squelched the thought. Either the buzz of the phone or Luke himself would have awakened her.

Pushing off the couch, she listened intently. She didn't hear any sounds. She assumed Luke was in the kitchen brewing the coffee. Before she faced him again, she needed to splash some cold water on her face.

Her stockinged feet made no sound as she mounted the curving oak staircase to the second floor. Open doors gave her glimpses into the rooms on both sides of the hall. Like the downstairs rooms, they were decorated with an eclectic mix of priceless antiques, comfortable furnishings and the best of Texas. One guest bedroom sported a canopy bed. Another, a huge four-poster that had to have come across Texas in a covered wagon.

Avoiding the master bedroom suite at the end of the hall, she made liberal use of the amenities in the well-stocked guest bathroom. Fifteen minutes later she headed back downstairs, face scrubbed, teeth clean and her bottle-blond hair tangle-free.

As she'd guessed, Luke was in the kitchen. It was a warm, welcoming place, one she remembered well. A beautiful old wrought-iron gate was suspended from chains above the center island, displaying an assortment of antique cast-iron frying pans, speckled tin cookware and a dented, ten-gallon coffeepot that had to have seen duty on the cattle trails. The cabinets were distressed cypress, reminding Haley of the trees that lined the creeks in this part of the country. Their glass fronts displayed an assortment of brightly colored crockery. A rectangular table of the same weathered cypress was set in an alcove surrounded on three sides by shuttered windows.

Luke sat at the table, with a cell phone close at hand and a laptop computer in front of him. Haley couldn't tell whether he'd slept at all or not, but he'd obviously showered. His cheeks and chin were smooth, and his black hair glistened. He'd changed into a crisp white cotton shirt with the sleeves rolled halfway up and a freshly laundered pair of jeans.

She made a futile attempt to smooth the wrinkles from her slept-in tank top before she remembered Luke couldn't see it. As soft as it was, the swish of her hands brushing down her front alerted him to her presence.

"Haley?" he asked sharply.

"I'm sorry. I didn't mean to sneak up on you. I'm in my socks."

"I heard the water running upstairs and figured you'd be down soon."

Neither one of them mentioned the fact that she'd fallen asleep in Luke's arms last night. He seemed as willing to dance around the topic as Haley was.

"The coffee's fresh, if you want some," he told her. "Mrs. Chavez won't be over to fix breakfast for another couple of hours, but she always leaves the fridge full if you need something to tide you over until then.''

At the mention of breakfast Haley's stomach sat up and took notice. She'd been so sick with worry over Lena and her father these past few days, the mere thought of food had made her nauseated. Her few hours sleep seemed to have restored her appetite, however. Taking advantage of Luke's invitation, she helped herself to coffee and downed several gulps while she surveyed the contents of the stainless-steel, commercial-grade fridge.

''Good grief! There are enough covered dishes in here to feed everyone in Mission Creek.''

''Yeah, I know,'' he drawled. ''Teresa is firmly convinced that all I need to regain twenty-twenty vision is rest and plenty of good, healthy food.''

Haley shot him a quick look. ''Any chance she's right?''

''Who knows?'' He rolled his shoulders under the white cotton shirt. ''The docs don't have any other advice to offer at this point.''

''Has there been any improvement at all since you came home?''

He hesitated, obviously unwilling to offer false hope to anyone, himself included.

''I'm seeing some shadows, mostly in contrast, They seem to be getting a little less dark and dense.

Probably just wishful thinking on my part. See anything that looks good in the fridge?''

Following his deliberate change of subject, she dragged her glance back to the neatly stacked containers. Each lid was labeled, she saw, marked with a thick plastic strip with raised letters so Luke could run his fingers over it and identify the contents.

''How does cinnamon toast and Mexican lasagna sound?''

''Pretty good.''

While the spicy tortilla, cheese and beef casserole heated in the microwave, Haley slathered thick slices of Texas toast with butter, sprinkled on cinnamon and popped them in the toaster oven. Her stomach rumbling in earnest now, she took the coffee carafe to the table to refresh Luke's cup as well as her own.

She felt awkward, as though they were strangers. Two people whose pasts had crossed and now shared only a single link to the future. Firmly suppressing the panic that fluttered just under her skin each time she though of Lena, she eyed the computer and its array of peripherals spread out in front of Luke.

''What's all this?''

''I've been making lists of what we need to do to get ready for Del Brio's call.''

It was Haley's turn to hesitate. She had little experience with physical disabilities and didn't want to harp on Luke's, but curiosity compelled her to ask how he could read what was on the computer screen.

"Obviously, I don't. The computer is specially rigged with raised-letter keys and voice recognition software for data input. It also produces both visual and audio output."

He tapped a key. A digitized voice filled the kitchen.

"Spence to retrieve ransom from bank. Two million. Unmarked, nonsequential bills. Flynt to attach microdots and scan bills into computer. Tyler to rig explosive in briefcase handle. Obtain spectrascope for—"

"Wait a minute!" Haley exclaimed. "What explosives?"

"—the SIG Sauer. Load high-velocity bullets. Test scope with—"

"Luke, turn that thing off!"

A quick click of a key cut off the electronic recitation. Shaken, Haley gripped her coffee cup with both hands. "What the heck is all this? Why are you making lists that include explosives and high-velocity bullets?"

"You don't think I intend to just hand the ransom to Del Brio and let him walk away, do you?"

"Yes! No!"

A frown gathered between his brows. "Which is it? What exactly did you have in mind, Haley?"

"Well, I haven't worked out the exact details yet. I thought maybe you could distract Frank while I got the drop on him."

"Right."

The sarcastic drawl raised her hackles.

"Look, I came to you to help me retrieve my baby. Our baby. I didn't expect you to mount a full-scale military offensive that might get her blown up, for God's sake!"

Luke started to reply, but cut off whatever he intended to say. His head cocked.

"Something's burning."

"Damn! The toast."

By the time Haley had scraped the black edges off the cinnamon bread and plunked it down on the table, she'd recovered a measure of her poise.

"We need to talk about this," she said with deliberate calm. "I appreciate that you feel the need to take an active role in Lena's recovery, but I won't let you endanger her."

"You won't, huh?"

Thrusting out his long legs, he sprawled back in his chair and fixed his gaze on her face. Although she knew he couldn't see her, Haley felt the full force of that penetrating stare.

"Seems to me you forfeited your rights to dictate what I can and can't do for my child when you abandoned her."

The warm, welcoming kitchen abruptly lost its glow.

"I'll repeat myself just one more time," Haley said, gritting her teeth. "I did not abandon her. I had to place Lena in safekeeping while I went undercover for the FBI. I thought you understood."

With a grimace of self-disgust, he nodded. "I do. I'm sorry. You didn't deserve that."

No, she didn't. Silence stretched out between them, broken by the sudden ping of the microwave. Luke pushed his chair back at the same time Haley rose.

"I'll get it," she muttered, still ruffled by the hostilities that had erupted so unexpectedly between them. Retrieving the casserole from the microwave, she let it steam on the stovetop while she located dishes, napkins and silverware.

"I'm left-handed," Luke said when she carried two well-filled plates to the table. "If you position the dish with the food at nine o'clock, I can eat without making too much of a mess."

"Right. Nine o'clock. Careful, it's hot."

The clipped reply told Luke she'd yet to forgive him for the attack a few minutes ago. Disgusted with himself for delivering such a swift counterpunch to what he'd interpreted as a lack of confidence in his ability to handle Frank Del Brio, he waited until she'd seated herself to make amends.

"You were right, Haley. I shouldn't be making lists or plans without consulting you. Nor should you be working up some wild scheme of your own. We're in this together, with a single goal. We need to work together as a team."

"Yes, we do."

Her relief was palpable. Luke felt it clear across the table.

"I called Flynt and Spence and Tyler last night," he told her. "They should be here within an hour or so. Before they arrive, I'll fill you in on what I think we can and should do, and you can give me what you know of the way Del Brio operates."

"That might take a while," she warned. "I've been gathering information on Frank and his cohorts for a year now."

"Then let's get to it."

Eleven

Haley soon discovered that Luke's idea of teamwork and hers differed considerably. He was used to being in charge and making things happen. She'd learned to live by her wits and to operate alone. As a result, they spent an hour at the kitchen table alternately sharing information, brainstorming possible scenarios for the ransom delivery and arguing about the best way to handle Frank Del Brio. They were still at it when Mrs. Chavez arrived.

Startled to find her employer sharing breakfast with a stranger, the housekeeper's curiosity gave way to openmouthed disbelief when Luke introduced her as the long-dead Haley Mercado.

"No, it cannot be!" She gaped at Haley, then emphatically shook her graying head. "You're joking with me, Luke."

"It's true. I just found out myself last night."

"But Haley Mercado drowned," the housekeeper exclaimed. "Right here in our lake." She turned a fierce frown on the intruder in her kitchen. "They found her body."

"I don't know who that poor woman was, but I'm very much alive."

Unconvinced, Teresa Chavez folded her arms and scowled. "You do not look at all like Haley Mercado."

"I had cosmetic surgery. Around the eyes and nose, mostly."

The housekeeper searched her face again, more intently this time. Haley saw disbelief give way to doubt, then to anger. Her scowl deepening, Teresa glared at Haley.

"My Luke and his friends stood trial. They almost went to prison because of you."

"Yes, I know."

"Haley wanted to come home during the trial," Luke said, surprising her by coming to her defense. "Judge Bridges assured her he'd get us off."

"Ah, Judge Bridges." The anger went out of the older woman's face. "So sad about the judge. And about your mother," she added, her glancing shifting once again to Haley. "It broke Isadora's heart when she thought she lost you."

"It broke my heart to let her think she had. I'm just glad I got to see her before she died."

The warmhearted housekeeper clucked in distress. "There has been so much death around Mission Creek of late. So much sadness. And now that little child is missing, the one my Luke says is his. Ayyyy, if I should ever meet the woman who walked off and left such a sweet little baby on the golf course, she would hear a thing or two from me, I can tell you that.''

Wincing, Haley prepared once again to shoulder the blame for the scheme the judge had assured her was infallible.

"Haley is the baby's mother," Luke said calmly.

Teresa's jaw dropped. "How can that be?"

He gave an expurgated version of their meeting two years ago and Haley's subsequent return after Lena's birth. Clucking her tongue again, the goggle-eyed housekeeper tried to take it all in. She was still trying when the intercom buzzed. Shaking her head, she went to the wall unit and pressed the speaker button.

"It's Spence, Teresa. Luke wants to see me. Let me in, will you?"

"Yes, yes. We are in the kitchen. Come around to the side door."

Haley used the few moments it took for Spence Harrison to pull his high-powered SUV up to the kitchen entrance to brace herself for another confrontation. She didn't know how much Luke had told the hard-edged former prosecutor, but she suspected he'd greet Haley Mercado's return from the dead with something less than wild enthusiasm.

Sure enough, the look Spence sent her when he entered the kitchen could have sliced through tempered steel. Hooking his thumbs in his belt, he ran a hard eye over the waitress who'd served him and his new wife at the country club.

Haley returned his narrow-eyed scrutiny. Marriage agreed with him, she thought. Spence had always been intense and, from what she'd heard through Carl Bridges during her years abroad, had made a hell of a prosecutor. Since his marriage to a single mom with a school-aged son, though, he'd given up the D.A.'s job to become a private law consultant and to spend more time with his new family. The change showed in his face. The lines were softer, the angles less sharp.

"I hear you've had a rough time of it," he said finally.

Haley had no answer for that.

"Luke explained why you disappeared the way you did. He also said you're Lena's mother." A rough sympathy glinted in his brown eyes. "We'll get her back."

She could have kissed him for putting aside the past and concentrating only on the urgent present.

"Thank you."

To her relief, at least one of the two men who

arrived a few moments later appeared ready to do the same. Tyler Murdoch tossed a small leather satchel onto the table and gave her a slow once-over, much as he had when she'd approached his table at the Saddlebag last night. The taciturn, one-time mercenary made no reference to her supposed drowning, however, and said only that he was there to help.

Flynt Carson seemed to have the toughest time accepting Haley's resurrection. Not because he, along with the three others, had been charged with her death. But because the ruggedly handsome rancher had taken Lena into his home and into his heart.

In her cover as Daisy Parker, Haley had ached inside every time Flynt and his wife, Josie, brought Lena into the country club and showed her off with such love and pride. She'd also seen that they were as shattered as Haley herself when the baby was kidnapped from their ranch four months ago. She fully expected Flynt to lay into her now for setting him and Josie up for that kind of pain. The regret she saw in his piercing blue eyes surprised her.

"You could have trusted us, Haley. Luke and I and the others would have helped you, both when you needed to escape Mission Creek and when you came back."

"I know I could trust you." A lump lodged in

her throat. "You were Ricky's closest friends. I had crushes on each one of you at various times. I just couldn't let you—any of you—put your lives at risk."

The brutal reality behind the statement silenced Flynt. Haley had nothing more to say, either. Shoving her hands into her jeans' pockets, she glanced from one man to the other.

How many times had she seen them standing shoulder to shoulder like this? How many times had she heard their shouts of laughter echoing through the Mercado house?

Luke. Spence. Tyler. Flynt.

And Ricky. If only Ricky were here! The Fabulous Five would be together again, guilt and blame forgotten, the past erased.

Maybe soon, she thought wearily. Now that she'd confessed the truth, maybe the five men could mend the broken links of their friendship. Maybe these four could pull Ricky from the pit he'd fallen into after Haley's supposed death. Clinging to that thin hope, she joined the group at the table. Teresa Chavez bustled around, serving coffee and the remains of her spicy stacked tortilla lasagna to the three hungry males before heading for the front of the house to make her morning rounds.

"Just to recap," Luke said, "Frank Del Brio

contacted Haley at an FBI safe house a little past nine last night and demanded two million dollars for Lena's safe return.''

"Did the FBI get a trace on the call?'' Tyler asked quickly.

"No.''

"Well, hell! What the heck kind of equipment are they using, anyway?''

"I don't know.''

"What kind of proof did he offer?'' Flynt put in. "How do we know Del Brio actually has Lena?''

"We don't, at this point. That's one of the conditions we'll stipulate. He'll have to deliver visual, real-time evidence that she's alive and unhurt before we deliver the two million.''

"Aren't you going to negotiate?'' Spence asked, frowning. "I hate to see scum like Del Brio make off with a cool two million.''

"Del Brio knows I'm good for it,'' Luke replied. "He won't settle for less and I don't want to waste time with lengthy negotiations. I want to get the money ready so Haley and I can deliver it to the specified point at the specified time.''

"Haley and you?''

Three pairs of eyes switched to the woman at the table. Tyler asked the question that showed clearly in each face. "Del Brio agreed to that?''

"No. He told me to make sure there were no cops or anyone who even faintly smells of FBI within fifty miles of the scene or I'd never—" Her voice hitched. "Or I'd never see Lena again. It was my idea to ask Luke for help."

"She figured Del Brio wouldn't consider me much of a threat," he explained wryly. "She also suggested I could provide some sort of distraction while she takes Del Brio down."

Haley braced herself, expecting Luke's three friends to become indignant on his behalf. To her surprise, they gave her plan serious consideration.

"She has a point there," Tyler mused, tapping his blunt-tipped fingers on the weathered wood of the table. "The little contact I've had with Frank over the years was enough to convince me that he's an arrogant bully. He wouldn't consider you a threat, Luke."

"If you play it right," Spence added slowly, "you might just get within range."

"That's what I'm counting on."

Luke's feral smile raised the small hairs on the back of Haley's neck. His three friends wore similar expressions. They'd closed ranks, she saw. Their shared training and military experience, not to mention the hardships they endured as POWs, had sent their minds racing along parallel tracks. Luke called on that experience now.

"Think you can fix me up, Tyler?"

"I've got a few tricks in my electronic grab bag that might just surprise ole Frank."

"Like what?" Haley asked. Her earlier argument with Luke had made her distinctly nervous. This one was adding to her uneasiness by the minute.

The mercenary shifted in his seat, obviously reluctant to lay out the tools of his trade. She leaned forward to make sure she had his full attention, as well as that of the other men at the table.

"Luke and I have already had this discussion, Tyler. We've agreed that we'll operate as a team. I don't want any surprises when we go to deliver the ransom. No wild pyrotechnics going off when I least expect them or explosive devices that might endanger my child."

Tyler still needed confirmation from their unspoken leader before he'd agree. "Luke?"

"Haley's right. She'll be out there on point with me when we deliver the ransom. She has to know who and what is backing her up."

"True," his friend conceded with a shrug. "Okay, here's what I'm thinking. We could outfit you with a miniaturized phased-array scanner. The army's testing one up at Fort Hood right now. It's the size of an ordinary wristwatch, but the damned thing sends out high-intensity radar waves, identifies objects that fit certain parameters and returns a perfect signature.''

''So Luke won't need sight to track Del Brio's every move,'' Spence put in for Haley's benefit. ''The scanner will do it for him.''

Tyler continued to outline his plan. ''I can also rig a special infrared laser scope that will lock on to a target and follow it. What weapons are you planning to take with you, Luke?''

''A SIG Sauer 9 mm. Maybe an ankle-holstered .38 Special, as well.''

Haley listened in a growing daze. They'd already moved so far beyond her original, half-formed plan using Luke as a distraction that she could scarcely keep up.

''What about explosives? I know where there's a stash of high-impact, zero-centered grenades.''

''No explosives,'' Luke said swiftly. ''At least not until Haley and Lena are well away from the scene. At which point,'' he added, ''there won't be enough left of Frank Del Brio to blow up.''

Tyler nodded. ''Good enough. I'll chopper up to Fort Hood as soon as we finish here and get working on this stuff.''

Nodding, Luke pushed a slip of paper across the table in Spence Harrison's general direction.

''Spence, I need you to retrieve the money for me. I e-mailed Hoyt Bennington last night and told him to expect you. Here's the authorization to withdraw the two million from my cash reserve account. Del Brio specified nonsequential bills, no larger than hundreds. Hoyt promised to have it banded and ready when you get there.''

"I'm on it.''

"Flynt?''

"Right here, buddy.''

"I don't plan to let Del Brio walk away with the ransom, but just in case, we'll have to tag the bills.''

"He insisted they had to be unmarked,'' Haley interjected.

"What Del Brio wants and what he gets are two different sacks of beans,'' Flynt drawled. "Don't worry. Tyler has a supply of some very interesting chemical agents. They can't be picked up by X-ray machines, light scanners or explosive-sniffing dogs. We'll treat the bills and, as backup, I'll also scan their serial numbers so we can send an alert through the Federal Reserve computers. If Del Brio walks with the cash, he won't walk far.''

"I don't know how much time we have,'' Luke warned the assembled team. "Del Brio could contact Haley at any time with instructions for delivery. We'll counter with a demand for proof of life, which should buy us at least a few hours, but we'll have to hustle.''

Chairs scraped the floor as the three friends rose.

"Not to worry," Tyler assured him. "We're off on our assigned tasks. We'll let you know if we run into any glitches. And just so Del Brio doesn't intercept our communications, we'd better use these."

Unzipping the leather satchel he'd tossed onto the table earlier, he passed out what looked to Haley like ordinary cell phones.

"They operate off a secure satellite and send scrambled signals," he explained. "The V.R.S.— Voice Recognition System—built into each phone restricts transmissions to only the person whose speech pattern the scrambler recognizes. Punch in 0-1-0-6 and say 'Mary had a little lamb' to activate the V.R.S."

Spence snorted. "'Mary had a little lamb'?"

"Hey, when Luke called late last night, Marisa and I were, uh, otherwise engaged. A nursery rhyme was the best I could come up with at the time."

"Considering that you and Marisa have been married for all of three weeks," Spence retorted, "I'm surprised he could get you out of bed at all."

"It took some doing," Luke drawled.

"What can I say?" the mercenary replied with a goofy grin. "I've finally been broken to the bit."

"From what Marisa's told me," Spence retorted, "you're a long way from being broken to the bit. But if anyone can do it, she can."

Silently, Haley agreed. She'd only crossed paths with Tyler's fiery, fiercely independent new wife a couple of times. The brief encounters had made a definite impression.

"I still can't believe all three of you went down in flames so quickly, one right after another." Shaking his head, Luke snapped closed the laptop's lid. "Single women all over the world are probably weeping as we speak."

The good-natured jab elicited a quick response from Flynt.

"You'll understand when you give up your free-wheeling bachelor ways," he predicted with the utter confidence of a man who, against all odds, had been given a second chance at love. His blue eyes flickered in Haley's direction before returning to his friend. "And in case you've forgotten, you've got a daughter to help raise now."

Haley stiffened. She wasn't prepared to discuss Luke's role in Lena's future. They'd work out the necessary arrangements if—when!—they got Lena back.

Luke evidently shared her reluctance to discuss the matter in front of his friends. Charging them to keep him posted on their progress during the next few hours, he sent them off on their various assignments.

With their exit, the intense energy levels that had swirled around the kitchen for the past hour seemed to drop a good ten or twenty amps. Suddenly Haley felt as drained. Pushing out of her chair, she started clearing the table of the plates and coffee mugs.

"You don't have to do that," Luke informed her. "Teresa has a helper who comes in. She'll take care of the dishes."

"I need to keep busy."

"Suit yourself." Tucking the laptop under his arm, he left her to her self-appointed task. "I'll be in the den."

Trailing his right hand along the marble countertop, he made his way out of the kitchen and down the hall. His footsteps echoed on the polished parquet floorboards. Belatedly, Haley realized the Persian runner that used to add such a glow of jewel-like colors to the hall was gone. Rolled up and stored away like the ones in the living room, she guessed, so Luke wouldn't trip over it.

Thinking how both their worlds had changed so dramatically, Haley collected the dirty dishes. A few minutes later she tucked the last of them into the dishwasher, wiped her hands on a handy towel and followed Luke to the den.

He was standing at the front windows, his hands shoved into his back pockets, staring through the sparkling panes as though he could actually see the glorious Texas morning now spreading its gold across the surface of the lake.

''What do we do now?'' she asked.

''We wait.''

Twelve

"Why doesn't he call?"

Clutching a dew-streaked iced-tea glass in a tight fist, Haley checked her watch. It was almost noon. Three and a half hours since Luke had sent his friends off on their appointed tasks. Fifteen since Frank Del Brio's call last night. She'd just about worn a rut in the den's hardwood floor with her pacing.

"He wants to keep you on edge," Luke stated calmly, following the sound of her voice.

"Well, he's doing a damned good job of it."

She'd been a bundle of nerves all morning. A call to the hospital assured her her father was holding his own. That had helped steady her, for a little while anyway. But the slow, dragging hours had piled tension on top of fear on top of frustration.

"He'll try to up the pucker factor until you won't stop to think when he does call, you'll just jump. Don't play into his hands, Haley. Sit down. Force yourself to relax."

"I can't make myself visualize a soft gray haze

right now,'' she muttered, too tense to attempt the relaxation technique that had worked so well last night. "I don't want to think about anything except Lena."

"So visualize her. Better yet, help me visualize her. Tell me about her."

The ploy worked. Haley's emotions shifted instantly from gnawing worry about her daughter to the remembered joy of cuddling her small, warm body. With a sigh, she dropped down in the overstuffed leather chair next to Luke's.

"She's so beautiful. Honestly! This isn't just a proud mother speaking. She's got fat little apple cheeks and the happiest gurgle. And she was born with the most incredible head of hair. Thick and black, like yours. The nurses tied a pink bow in it the day we left the hospital."

Swirling the ice in her watered-down tea, Haley savored the memory. What could have been such a wrenching experience for a single woman had in fact been the most momentous event of her life.

"She has your eyes, too. At least she did the last time I saw her," she added with a hitch in her voice. "That was four months ago. Four months! She was just coming up on her first birthday."

"Is that the magic point?" Luke asked, dragging her back from the brink again with his deliberate calm. "One year? After that, a baby's eye color doesn't change?"

"Not if the books I read are right. Supposedly the pigment cells in the irises accumulate and the eye color matures by the time the baby's a year old."

"So she's got my hair and eyes. What did she inherit from you?"

"My stubbornness," Haley replied without hesitation. "For such a tiny bit of fluff, she's got a temper she doesn't mind showing every so often. She has my skin tone, too, compliments of her Italian heritage. Her nose is still just a button, thank goodness. I'm hoping she doesn't develop the little bump in the bridge my mother passed on to me. I didn't miss that when the cosmetic surgeon gave me a new nose."

"The surgeon did a good job. I remember thinking you looked familiar when you first walked into the Saddlebag that night. I couldn't place you, but there was something. Your walk maybe, or the way you held yourself. But I knew I'd never seen your face before. I would have remembered it. What do you look like now?"

With a start, Haley remembered he'd never seen her in her Daisy Parker persona. He'd left the country just before she began her stint as a waitress at the country club. When he returned, he'd lost his sight.

"I have the same face I did that night at the Saddlebag. I just use a lot more makeup."

Or she had, until the shoot-out three nights ago that left her father in ICU and Haley buttoned up in the FBI's safe house. She'd hardly eaten or slept since, let alone bothered with makeup.

"When I first went undercover, I had injections to make my lips fuller. I've lost weight these past months, too. Except for my hair, which is a lighter blond now, I'm pretty close to the woman I was two years ago."

She hesitated, then placed her glass on a coaster and slipped out of her chair to sit on her heels beside his. Reaching for his left hand, she guided it to her cheek.

"Do you recognize that woman, Luke?"

The roughened pads of his fingers moved across her cheek to her nose. With a small frown of concentration, he followed the smooth slope down and up again before tracing the line of her brows. Leaning forward, he brought his right hand up to join the left. His palms cupped her cheeks. His thumbs moved over her lips in slow exploration.

Haley's breath caught. His touch was light and gentle, but her skin prickled with each slow stroke. He was so close to her now, his elbows resting on his knees, his face mere inches from her own as he rediscovered the woman whose mouth and body he'd claimed repeatedly the night they'd conceived their child.

At the memory of those stolen hours Haley felt her womb clench in a spasm of pure sexual need. She hadn't been with another man since that night with Luke, hadn't felt the least desire for someone else's touch.

She closed her eyes, determined to level the playing field with Luke. With each quiver of her nostrils she took in the faint, lime-scented tang of his aftershave. With each brush of his thumbs along her lips she tasted herself on his skin. She heard his breathing quicken, roughen. Felt his hands slide to her nape.

Sensation after sensation crashed through her. Her belly clenched again, lower, harder. Liquid heat poured into her veins. Two years of pent-up emotion burst through the dike. She could scarcely breathe. Part of it, she knew, was sheer relief that he'd put the past behind them and agreed to help her get Lena back. Another part—deeper, more visceral—was the want she'd carried with her for as long as she could remember. The want that had led her to take his hand that night at the Saddlebag. Hunger arced through her. Fierce. Unrelenting.

He pulled her closer, communicating his own

need in a way that drew an instinctive response. Rising up her knees, she looped her arms around his neck and brought her mouth to his.

After the first startled instant, he got into the kiss. His mouth slanted over hers, as hard and hungry as Haley's was warm and willing.

She was breathless when she finally sank back on her heels. Eyes wide open now, she stared up at his face and tried to rein in her wildly galloping thoughts. Luke got his under control before she did.

"Yep," he said with a wry halfsmile. "You're most definitely the woman you were two years ago. And more, Haley. One helluva lot more."

She had no idea how to respond to that. Thankfully she didn't have to. The intercom buzzed at that moment, ripping through the sensual haze enveloping her. Startled, she twisted around, lost her balance and ended up in a heap on the floor beside Luke's chair.

The intercom buzzed again, three short, impatient jabs, before he got to it.

"It's Spence, Luke. Flynt's with me. We've got the cash and a high-speed scanner. Open the gates."

Haley hadn't stopped to consider how many hundred-dollar bills it would take to meet Del

Brio's ransom demand. Her eyes widened as Spence opened a well-worn leather case and dumped its contents onto the kitchen table.

"There you are," the former D.A. announced. "Twenty thousand hundred-dollar bills, banded in bundles of ten thousand dollars each."

"Twenty thousand bills!" Haley gasped. Four faces swung in her direction. "Sorry," she murmured. "I didn't do the math. Tell me what to do."

"Your job is to unband a bundle and fan out the bills so I can run this optical scanning wand over the serial numbers. Flynt will man the laptop and make sure the data enters correctly. Then you pass the bills to Luke and he'll mark a corner of each with this stuff Tyler left us."

The "stuff" came in an unmarked, quart-size plastic container. It gave off a light, almost fruity odor when Spence unscrewed the lid and carefully filled a tubelike marker with a pinpoint sponge tip.

"I don't understand," Haley said. "If we're scanning in the serial numbers, why is it necessary to mark the bills, as well?"

"Federal Reserve banks have the personnel and the resources to conduct periodic screens of serial numbers," Spence explained. "They can help authorities track dispersal patterns across the country over an extended period of time. For quicker results, we're treating the bills with a chemical that reacts instantly when exposed to the kind of fluorescent lights used in department and grocery stores.''

The lawyer's mouth curved in a wicked grin. ''If you think that stuff smells distinctive now, you should take a whiff of it once it's been exposed to fluorescent lighting.''

''Del Brio may pass one or two of the bills,'' Luke said with grim satisfaction. ''That's all he'll pass. Okay, folks, let's get to it.''

It was slow work. Physical, too. Haley had kept in shape the past twelve months hauling heavy trays and working ten- to twelve-hour shifts, but her back soon sent out warning signals each time she bent over to fan the bills.

Teresa Chavez came in a half hour after they got started. When she saw her kitchen table carpeted in hundred-dollar bills, her eyes bugged out. She didn't have to be told what they were doing, though. Luke had already informed her of the ransom demand.

''How can I help?'' the housekeeper asked.

''We've got a good routine going,'' Luke replied, ''but we're sure working up an appetite. You could rustle us up some lunch.''

With a start, Haley realized her breakfast of cinnamon toast and Mexican lasagna had long since worn off. With the same enthusiasm as the men she fell on the coleslaw, thick-slabbed ham sandwiches and baked beans Teresa produced. After tucking the hearty meal under their belts, they went back to work with renewed energy.

They'd marked almost a fourth of the bundles when the phone rang. Everyone at the table froze. Their eyes cut instantly to flickering red light on the cordless house phone.

Luke rapped out two swift commands. "Flynt, get on the extension in my office. Teresa, let it ring twice more before you answer it."

The rancher sprang out of his chair. The housekeeper gulped and moved toward the cordless phone.

"Damn," Spence muttered as the phone shrilled a second time. "We should have had Tyler rig a tracking device on your house phones."

"Haley and I talked about that," Luke replied grimly. "Del Brio's too smart to stay on the line long enough to work a trace. He proved that last night. I've hooked up a recorder, though. I'll get—"

He broke off at the third ring. Cocking his head, he listened intently as Teresa punched the talk button on the cordless phone.

"Callaghan residence." Her dark eyes shifted to Haley. "Yes, she's here."

Sick certainty curled in Haley's stomach. It was Frank. It could only be Frank.

"Who may I say's calling?"

The reply sent red rushing into the housekeeper's cheeks. Her lips folded into a thin line, she marched across the room and held out the phone.

"This *malhechor* says he's your fiancé."

Haley jammed the phone to her ear with a white-knuckled fist. "Is Lena all right? Is she there with you?"

Frank's chuckle floated over the line. "She's here, babe. Right beside me."

"How do I know you're not lying?"

"What, you want me to pinch her or something to make her squeal?"

"No!" The idea of Frank bruising her baby's delicate skin made her frantic. "No, please! Don't hurt her!"

With a smothered oath, Luke reached across the table and pried the phone out of her hand. "This is Callaghan, Del Brio."

"Well, well. So she came to you for the money, did she?"

"You know damned well she did or you wouldn't have called here."

"Don't get smart with me, Callaghan. I'm the one holding all the cards in this hand." Sloughing off his false geniality like a snake shedding its skin, Del Brio switched gears. "Rumor is you're the brat's father. That true?"

"Yes."

"Have you and Haley been getting it on all this time? Were you doing her when she was wearing my ring?"

There was more than anger behind the questions. There was an overlay of sick, twisted jealousy. Luke made a mental note of both before replying.

"If I was, she wouldn't have been wearing your ring. You couldn't keep her then, and you're sure as hell not going to have another chance at her."

"What, you think you're gonna get between us, you blind, useless cripple? I don't think so. I've seen the way your friends lead you around like a puppy on a leash. Haley needs a real man."

"Like you?"

"Yeah, like me. She's mine, Callaghan. You hear me? You might have slipped past me once when I wasn't looking, but I'm telling you now, I'm going to—"

"You're going to what, Del Brio?"

As if realizing how much of himself he'd exposed, he abruptly switched topics. "You got the two million?"

"I've got it, but you won't see a penny until we have proof Lena's alive and well."

"Proof? You want proof? All right, I'll give you proof. I'll send you one of the brat's fingers."

"Cut the crap, Del Brio. You're a businessman. You wouldn't pay for damaged goods and neither will I. Send proof, then we'll talk."

With a click of a button, Luke cut the connection.

Absolute silence followed. Spence frowned in intense concentration. Teresa Chavez stared at her employer. Haley sat in stunned shock.

She cleared her throat. Slowly. Painfully. Even then, all she could manage was a hoarse croak. "Damaged goods? Were you talking about Lena?"

Luke smothered a curse. He could hear the near panic she was fighting to control. For a second or two he considered glossing over Del Brio's threat. Just as swiftly he discarded the idea. He and Haley were in this together. A team. Besides, she'd probably insist on listening to the tape of the call.

"Del Brio wasn't happy when I said he wouldn't get his money until we received proof Lena was still alive. He said he'd send one of her fingers."

Haley gave a small, strangled sound. Teresa's was louder and sharper.

"Ayyyy!" Her face contorting, the housekeeper made the sign of the cross three times in rapid succession. "That poor little baby!"

"He was bluffing."

"How do you know that?" Fury broke through Haley's incipient panic. "How can you know that?"

"I know."

"That's not good enough, damn you! If Frank harms my daughter, I'll never forgive you."

"She's my daughter, too," Luke fired back, gripped by the savage need to hunt Del Brio down and skin him alive. "Do you think I'd deliberately goad someone into mutilating my child?"

"How do I know what you'd do? We've spent exactly one night together in over a decade!"

"Two, if you count last night."

"Well, I don't! I mean, last night wasn't— We didn't— Oh, hell!" The air escaped from her lungs like a deflating balloon. "Do you really think Lena will be all right?"

"Yes, I do. I also think we can expect Frank to deliver something within the next few hours. You guys get back to work while I make a quick call."

Luke joined Flynt in the den he'd converted to a modern, functional office. Fitted with flat workspaces and ample storage cabinets, it contained an array of computer and electronic wizardry that would have made Bill Gates drool. The gadget attached to the phone was the one that had caught Flynt's attention.

"What's this small flat disc?"

"It's a scrambler. Ordinarily it would be buried within the instrument itself, but I'm testing a new system for some folks in Washington."

"I though you were finished with that business."

"I am, pretty much."

"After getting blown all to hell and back, you should damned well cut the tie completely."

"You never cut the tie completely."

Not with OP-12, anyway. Even a blind operative had his uses. Particularly one with Luke's years of experience.

Flynt grumbled under his breath, clearly not happy. He and Spence still hadn't quite forgiven Luke for never once clueing them in about his years with OP-12. Tyler came closer to understanding. He'd left the marines to freelance, assuming a sort of quasi-official status with the covert military agency he worked for. Still, even Tyler had been stunned when he'd learned his playboy pal Luke Callaghan had spearheaded an ultrasecret, multinational thrust deep in the Mezcayan jungle to rescue their old commander, Colonel Phillip Westin.

After the rescue attempt went bad and Luke lost

his sight, Tyler had stepped in—but not before ripping a strip a mile wide off his friend for keeping his three buddies in the dark all these years.

Well, those years lay behind Luke now. His only contribution to OP-12 these days was to test equipment and, when requested, to offer operational advice. He hadn't lost his clout in the organization, though. After verification of his identity by code and by voice recognition, he was put right through to the acoustics branch.

"I need a full analysis run on the call just received at this number," he told the branch chief.

"You got it," the woman at the other end of the line replied.

"I want it quick."

"How quick?" she asked warily.

"Like yesterday."

The cheerful mother of three with double Ph.D.s in mechanical and audio engineering laughed. "So what else is new? I'll get back to you within an hour."

The branch chief had been with OP-12 almost as long as Luke had. From past experience, he knew she was as good as her word.

That task done, he ran a hand along the work surface until he located the recorder hooked up to the phone. Frowning, he ejected the CD Rewritable disc and hefted it in the palm of his hand. The conversation burned onto it was already etched into his mind.

"Did you catch that bit about Haley still belonging to Del Brio?" he asked Flynt.

"Yeah, I did. I also noticed that he still refers to himself as her fiancé." The rancher let a couple of seconds tick by. "Are you thinking maybe ole Frank is more interested in getting his hands on Haley Mercado than on the ransom?"

"That's exactly what I'm thinking."

Thirteen

Spence agreed with Flynt and Luke's assessment. So did Tyler when he returned from his trip to Fort Hood a half hour later and listened to the recorded call. His face thoughtful, he strolled back into the kitchen, which had become their unofficial command center, and addressed the small group.

"Well, this certainly alters our approach. Sounds like we need to plan for a possible snatch and run, not just a recovery operation."

His glance drifted to Haley. She sat at the table working her bundles of hundreds, but the call from Frank had shaken her so much that she couldn't regain the smooth rhythm she'd established previously.

Was Luke right? Was Frank more interested in getting his hands on her than on the ransom? The possibility made her physically ill, but she'd give herself to Del Brio in a heartbeat in exchange for Lena's safety.

"Actually, a snatch and run makes things simpler," Tyler mused. "I was worried Del Brio would send someone else to pick up the ransom. From the drift of that call, I'm betting he'll insist Haley deliver the ransom to him personally.''

"In which case," Luke put in, his face granite-hard, "he'll have to use the baby as enticement to make sure she shows.''

"Exactly." Tyler's brown eyes locked on Haley. "You were right. Looks like you're going to be out there on point, after all. Sure you're up to it?''

"I've been 'out there' for over a year," she reminded him. "I'm up to it.''

Admiration flickered across his tanned face. "Yeah, I guess you are.''

Luke didn't miss the subtle change in the tenor of the conversation. Nor the way his friends were now responding to Haley. Like him, they'd greeted the news of her return to the realm of the living with stunned disbelief, confusion and a healthy jolt of anger. Luke wasn't the only one who'd carried a load of guilt around all these years.

And like Luke, the three men had swiftly worked past their anger. They now understood the reason for her desperate flight. They were beginning to understand, too, the incredible courage it took for her to return to Mission Creek to go undercover as Daisy Parker.

She had that in spades, Luke admitted silently.

Courage, smarts and a sensuality that acted on him like a cattle prod every time he got within touching distance of her. He'd just about lost it earlier this afternoon in the den. One kiss, and he'd been ready to stretch her out on the floor. Hell, just thinking about the feel of her mouth under his had him itching to tell his buddies to hit the road.

"How did you make out up at Fort Hood?" he asked Tyler, forcing himself to concentrate on the matter at hand.

"Like a kid in a candy shop! Man, you wouldn't believe the toys those guys are playing with up there. I sure as hell wouldn't want to get on the bad side of the United States military these days."

"I don't think anyone else does, either," Flynt put in. "Our guys have sure kicked ass recently."

"Particularly the Fourteenth Marines," Spence added with savage satisfaction.

For a moment the four friends shared a tight, fierce loyalty to their former unit. Only those who'd experienced combat could understand the almost indestructible bond it forged between comrades-in-arms.

Almost indestructible. The fact that one of their group was missing still gnawed at Luke. Where the hell was Ricky? He had to know by now Frank suspected his sister was still alive. Had to guess Del Brio had kidnapped her baby to lure her out of hiding. Had he been secretly involved in the shoot-out three nights ago, when Del Brio slipped through the FBI net? Was he, too, on the run?

Tyler broke into his troubled thoughts. "You and I should go down to the lake, buddy. We need to test this little hummer. Make sure it works as advertised."

"Right." Turning toward the woman whose scent and warmth now acted like a beacon in the shadows, Luke offered what reassurance he could. "I'll take the phone with me. If Del Brio calls, let me handle him. He knows he can use your worry for Lena to twist you into knots."

"Do you think we'll hear from him soon?"

The best he could do was a shrug. "As he said, he's holding most of the cards right now. We'll hear from him when he's ready."

The next contact from Frank didn't come until ten-fifteen that night.

Spence, Flynt and Tyler had left some hours earlier. They'd offered to stay, but the bills were marked, the serial numbers scanned, and Luke had been thoroughly checked out on the wristwatch-size phased-array radar that gave him a startlingly accurate return signature.

He'd also received the promised return call from OP-12. Acoustics had run every analysis in the book, but could provide only limited information. The call was made at a pay phone located within a half mile of a major highway. Semis had roared by in the distance. The acoustics wizards had also detected the sound of a tractor, which narrowed the area some, given that this was primarily range country.

Luke contacted the FBI and passed the information to Sean Collins, along with a scathing rebuke for not reading him on Daisy Parker's identity. Doggedly unapologetic, Collins agreed with Luke's insistence that they share all information from here on out.

"Sheriff Wainwright's here with me," the agent informed Luke. "He's offered the entire resources of his department to help."

"Tell Justin I appreciate the offer," Luke said sincerely. He hated having to cut out the man who'd risked his life, alongside his wife, in the abortive attempt to rescue Lena. But Del Brio had been adamant. So had Haley. This was their operation now, hers and Luke's.

Haley listened to the exchange in silence and resumed the pacing she'd begun earlier this afternoon. Luke finally convinced her to go upstairs and indulge in a long, hot soak.

Twenty minutes later the computer in his office pinged, announcing the arrival of an e-mail.

Counting his steps in the way that had become second nature to him now, Luke navigated the short distance to his office. A quick click with the mouse took him to his e-mail program. Another click activated the speech component. An instant later Del Brio's voice leapt out at him.

"You wanted proof, Callaghan. Here it is."

A series of soft pings indicated that the computer was downloading an image. Eyes narrowed, Luke strained every nerve in his body in an effort to make out the picture on the screen. All he could distinguish was a hazy blur of dark on light.

Swearing viciously, he sat staring at the screen. He'd never regretted the loss of his vision more than he did at this moment. He couldn't see his own child. Didn't know whether she was laughing or crying or lying in a pool of blood.

His spine locked, shoulders roped with tension, he waited for Haley to come downstairs. He heard her flip-flopping down the hall some fifteen minutes later.

"I raided your closet for some slippers and one of your shirts. I hope you don't mind."

Consumed with the need to know what was on the screen, Luke barely registered the faint combination of starched cotton and lemony shampoo that came into the office with her.

"I didn't hear the phone ring."

"Del Brio chose another communication medium this time. I've been waiting for you to look at this."

Slippers flopping, she rushed forward and bent over his shoulder. Luke could feel her body tremble where it contacted his, and the kink in his gut took another vicious twist. He hated not being able to prepare Haley for what she might see on the screen.

"Dear God, that's Lena!"

She'd never know how much it took to keep his voice level and calm. "How does she look?"

"Happy. Oh, Luke, she looks happy." Giddy with relief, she drummed a fist on his shoulder. "She's clutching a fluffy stuffed rabbit and she's laughing at the camera."

Some of the tension holding Luke in a rigid brace seeped out of his spine. He relaxed, leaning back in his chair. The slight movement brought the back of his head in direct contact with the warm, soft swell of Haley's breasts. With a vicious effort, he blanked his mind to the sensations that raced through him.

"Describe the background details. What do you see in the image besides Lena?"

"She's sitting on the floor in front of a TV. It looks like there's some kind of a news show on. CNN's 'Headline News,' I think. Yes, it's 'Headline News.' I can see the banner at the bottom of the screen.''

"Does it show a time and date?''

"Yes. Today's date. The time is...''

She leaned closer to the screen. Luke felt himself begin to sweat.

"The time is seven thirty-six. Only a little over three hours ago!''

"Computer images are easy to doctor,'' he cautioned, hating to douse the joy and relief in her voice. "I doubt if this one was, since Frank knows we'll check it out. Still, it won't hurt to have a few experts take a look at it.''

"No, it won't. Just print me a copy, will you?''

While his high-tech laser color printer whirred, Luke composed a brief message to a nameless, faceless entity in a building outside McLean, Virginia, and hit the send key. Next, he tapped out a quick e-mail to Special Agent Sean Collins at the FBI command center. Extracting the printed copy of the photo, he swung his chair around. She chose the same moment to lean across him and reach for the photo herself.

Luke's shoulder caught her square in her ribs. Off balance, she stumbled sideways and would have fallen if Luke hadn't grabbed for her. One hand contacted starched cotton. The other, bare skin. With an adroit maneuver he managed to convert her fall into an awkward tumble that brought her into his lap. She landed with a little plop and a shaky laugh.

"Good catch, Callaghan. Thanks."

"You're welcome."

He fully intended to remove his hand from her bare thigh. In a minute. Curling his palm around the smooth flesh, he held her balanced on his knees.

"Sorry about the body block. I didn't hurt you, did I?"

"No, you didn't."

Luke half expected her to wiggle off his lap. She had to feel the heat she was raising in him. Hell, his hand burned like a brand where it wrapped around the silk of her inner thigh. Drawn by the fire, he slid his palm up another inch or so.

She made a queer little breathy sound, louder than a sigh, softer than a gasp. "Luke?"

His hand stilled. "Yes?"

"About that kiss in the living room this afternoon..."

"What about it?"

"I didn't plan it."

"I know. I wasn't planning on this one, either."

He managed to find her lips with only minimal bumping of chins and noses. Her head tipped back to improve the contact, bunching her still-wet hair against his shoulder. Luke registered the dampness through his shirt for a moment or two before her mouth opened under his. With a grunt of sheer male satisfaction, he shifted her higher on his lap.

The small movement tipped Haley's soaring emotions over the edge. She was ecstatic at seeing evidence her baby was happy. Overwhelmed by all Luke was doing to help rescue Lena. If she hadn't ached for him before, the feelings he roused in her now would have done the trick.

Joy swiftly became hunger. Relief crashed into need. Want left her mindless of the oversize shirt falling off her shoulders. Her mouth turned greedy, her hands even more so as she slid her palms over his chest and shoulders.

Luke's greed matched hers. She could feel him straining against her, under her. Taking full advantage of the now widely gaping shirt, he found her breast. The calloused pads of his palm raised shivery sensations against her skin. Within moments his busy fingers had brought her nipple to an aching peak.

"I've carried a picture of you in my head since that night at the Saddlebag," he muttered, hitching her up another few inches. "I remember your mouth soft and swollen from my kisses. Your nipples dusky red and stiff."

"You'd better hang on to that mental image,"

she said on a shaky laugh. "I've aged a bit since then. I've also had a baby. I have the stretch marks to prove it."

"Do you? Where? Here?"

His hand slid down, charting a path past the starched folds of the shirt. Haley's stomach quivered at the exploratory touch. She wasn't wearing panties. She'd washed out the pair she'd had on when she'd rushed out to find Luke. They were upstairs, draped over the shower rod in the guest bathroom alongside her bra.

Luke obviously approved of the omission. After only a stroke or two, he abandoned his search for stretch marks and found the heat between her legs. The heel of his hand exerted an exquisite pressure on her mound, while his thrusting fingers nearly carried her to climax. Embarrassed, Haley clenched her legs and tried frantically to stem the tidal wave of sensations.

"Luke, wait! It's been two years!"

She hadn't intended to provide that particular item of information. It just slipped out, along with every bit of breath in her lungs as he deliberately, wickedly increased the pressure.

"Are you saying you're too out of practice?" he asked, nipping at her neck.

"No. I'm saying I'm too ready."

Laughter puffed against her throat. "Oh, sweetheart, that's the last thing you should tell a man when you want him to stop.''

''Who said I want you to stop?''

Wriggling like a stranded fish, Haley twisted around and straddled his thighs. They were face-to-face now. Breath-to-breath.

''What I want,'' she informed him, yanking at his belt buckle, ''is to feel you inside me.''

His breath snagged. His belly hollowed. With a growl he shoved aside her fumbling hands and freed himself from his jeans. She was wet when he lifted her hips, and ready, so ready, when he entered her in a smooth, sure thrust.

They made wild, greedy love in his office before moving to Luke's king-size bed for a slower, more deliberate joining. He positioned the phone on the nightstand within easy reach in case Frank called, then took Haley to magical places, where she almost—almost—forgot Del Brio altogether.

Limp and totally sated, she nestled her head on Luke's shoulder and let her sleepy gaze roam his bedroom. As the rest of the house, it was furnished with an eye to masculine comfort blended with family antiques and Texas treasures. Stressed leather covered three walls above the waist-high paneling. Bookshelves took up the fourth, with a Remington bronze occupying the place of honor in a specially lighted central niche. An iron bootjack sat beside an oversize arm chair and served a necessary purpose.

It was a man's room, she thought, yet one a woman could feel cherished in. All it needed was a few feminine touches. Sweet-scented potpourri instead of cigars in the humidor on the bedside table, maybe. Her clothes hanging opposite Luke's in that cavernous walk-in closet.

With a frown she brought her thoughts to a jerky halt. She was getting ahead of herself here. Way ahead of herself. She shut down that treacherous line of thought, only to discover Luke was doing some thinking of his own.

"Haley?"

"Mmm?"

"All those years in London you never found anyone to hold you and keep you safe?"

"I wasn't looking."

"Why not?"

"At first I was too nervous. I kept pretty much to myself until I got comfortable in my new identity. Even then I allowed myself only a small circle of friends."

"There wasn't anyone special?"

Only you.

Not ready to admit how often Luke Callaghan had figured in her private dreams all those years,

Haley merely shrugged. He wasn't ready to let the matter drop, though. Stroking her hair, he continued his probe.

"Why did you go with me that night at the Saddlebag?"

"Seeing my mother so bruised and battered shook me, Luke. Badly. I'd never felt more alone than I did that night. Or more lonely."

"So you went with me out of loneliness?"

"Yes. Partly."

"Only partly?"

Slipping out from under his hand, she raised up on one elbow. "What do you want me to say? That I needed a man?"

"Well, I was hoping for something more specific. Like maybe you needed me."

"Okay, maybe I did. Does that make a difference?"

"Yeah, it does."

"Why?"

"Because I'm beginning to think the feeling was mutual. It's hard to put into words, but after you drowned— After you left," he amended hastily, "I kept a part of myself hidden, too."

"From what I read in the tabloids," Haley said dryly, "you didn't exactly lack for companionship."

"I didn't. But I never felt the need I felt that night at the Saddlebag."

"Are you saying you were lonely, too? That's what brought you over to my table that night?"

"Partly," he said, echoing her earlier reply.

She struggled to adjust her mental image of the man Luke Callaghan had been with one who'd lived with as many secrets as Haley had herself. She wasn't quite there when his mouth curved in a wicked grin.

"The other part," he confessed, dragging her down for a kiss, "was pure lust."

Fourteen

The next morning Haley lingered in the guest bathroom long after she'd showered and blow-dried her hair. Luke had given her first crack at the master bath, but she'd opted for the one down the hall she'd already more or less claimed as her own. She needed some space—and some privacy—to sort through her confusion.

Funny what a difference a few hours could make.

Last night she'd tumbled into Luke's arms without a thought for the complications or the consequences that might follow. Just as she'd done two years ago. This morning she was having second, third, and fourth doubts. Just as she'd done two years ago.

"Talk about your slow learners," she muttered, plucking a few blond strands from her comb and tossing them in the wicker wastebasket.

How could she make such a fool of herself twice with the same man? Thank goodness she'd stopped short of telling him the real reason she'd gone with him that night at the Saddlebag. She could just imagine his reaction if she'd admitted that she'd loved him for as long as she could remember.

He, on the other hand, had been right up front with her. He'd been feeling a touch of loneliness two years ago. And a whole lot of lust. Love hadn't figured into things that night. Nor did it come into play now.

On his side of the equation, anyway.

Time Haley accepted that basic fact and hauled her butt downstairs. She had more pressing concerns to worry about, chief among them her daughter. Plunking the comb down on the marble vanity, she followed the scent of fresh-brewed coffee to the kitchen.

Luke stood at the center island, a coffee mug in hand. Glancing up, he zeroed in on her with such pinpoint accuracy that Haley forgot he couldn't actually see her. Self-consciously, she tugged at the hem of the pale blue shirt she'd borrowed from him. Even with the sleeves rolled up, she swam in the cloud-soft cotton.

"I should make a run to my apartment," she said by way of greeting. "If Frank doesn't call soon with instructions on when and where to deliver the ransom, I'll deplete your entire wardrobe."

"It's safer for you here. Make a list of the items

you need and I'll have someone pick them up for you.''

The clipped response lifted Haley's brows. From the sound of it, she wasn't the only one experiencing a few morning-after doubts.

"All right. Have you had breakfast?"

"Just coffee. I'm not hungry. Help yourself to whatever you want.''

"Just coffee will do for me, too."

She joined him at the island, filled another mug and took a cautious sip.

"We need to talk about last night, Haley."

The sip turned into a gulp. Hastily she downed the too hot brew. "Yes, I guess we do."

"I don't usually make that kind of mistake."

His words burned worse than the scalding coffee. Carefully she placed her mug on the granite counter. "You consider last night a mistake?"

"Hell, yes. Don't you?"

"I'm beginning to."

Grimacing at her strained reply, he shook his head. "You can't blame me any more than I blame myself. If I'd acted as irresponsibly in the field as I did last night, I would have come home in a box.''

He slid his hand along the counter and found hers. His grip was warm and, she supposed, intended to be reassuring.

"I'm sorry, Haley. I know worry over Lena has kept you on a constant roller coaster ride. I felt your burst of relief after seeing her picture last night and knowing she was happy and well cared for." The disgust came back into his face. "I can't believe I took advantage of your emotional vulnerability that way."

"You think that's why I fell all over you? Out of relief?"

"Didn't you?"

"Okay, maybe some. But there were other emotions involved. Like that lust we talked about. I wanted you, Luke."

"I wanted you, too. So bad, I hurt with it." He squeezed her hand. "But this is one of those intense situations where things get distorted easily."

"I seem to be a little slow this morning. What exactly have we distorted?"

"Nothing, yet. I'm just saying the potential is there. Look, Haley, you know I'll do whatever it takes to get Lena back safely. Once that's accomplished, I don't want you to feel obligated in any way or think you're tied to a…" His mouth twisted down at one side. "How did Del Brio put it? To a blind, useless cripple."

The irony took Haley's breath away. Here she'd been writhing inside, worrying Luke had sensed that her feelings for him went far deeper than want, thinking he was warning her off.

Evidently he was, but for an entirely different reason than the one she'd postulated. She hadn't considered, hadn't remotely imagined, that his impaired vision might be a factor.

"Is that what this is all about?" she asked incredulously. "Your sight, or lack of it?"

"It has to be considered."

"You idiot! Of course it does. But not in any discussion about last night or how we might or might not feel after we get our baby back."

His black brows slashed down. The look on his face wavered between surprise and a scowl. Obviously, Luke Callaghan wasn't used to being contradicted. Too wound up to soothe his ruffled feelings, Haley tugged her hand free of his.

"You're right about one thing, though. In a situation like this, things can easily become distorted. Why don't we drop the whole topic of last night? For now, anyway."

After his little noble speech he could hardly refuse. His scowl lingered, however, as they downed the rest of their coffee.

It was still there, feathering around the edges of his mouth, when Mrs. Chavez bustled into the kitchen just before eight, followed in short order by Spence Harrison, Flynt Carson, Tyler Murdoch and their wives. In the space of mere minutes, the atmosphere in the kitchen went from intense to chaotic.

"Sorry, buddy." Ruefully, Flynt explained the sudden invasion. "When I got home last night, Josie guessed something was up. I told her about the call from Del Brio. She told Ellen, who in turn relayed the news to Marisa."

"Yes," the statuesque Marisa Rodriguez Murdoch said with a toss of her glorious, blue-black hair, "and we are not happy, Josie and Ellen and I, that our men are such fools they did not tell us sooner so we could come and help."

Wisely, the three fools in question kept their mouths shut and let Luke take full blame.

"Sorry. That was my doing. I asked them to keep this operation as close-hold as possible."

"If you think we women couldn't assist," the fiery Spanish interpreter snapped, "then you, too, are a fool."

"Funny," Luke drawled. "That seems to be the general consensus this morning."

Brushing past her husband, slender, vivacious Josie Lavender Carson crossed the kitchen. She'd met Haley only in her cover as a waitress at the Lone Star Country Club and was still obviously astounded at her real identity.

"I couldn't believe it when Flynt told me you're Ricky Mercado's sister. And Lena's mother."

Haley stiffened, expecting reproach from the nanny Flynt had hired to care for the baby he and the others had found on the golf course, but Josie's emerald-green eyes held only sympathy.

"It must have killed you all those months to see me holding and cuddling your child."

"It did," Haley confessed. "The only thing that kept me from snatching her out of your arms was knowing she was loved and well cared for."

"Now that I have a baby of my own," the new mother said gently, "I appreciate the courage it took for you to do what you did."

Ellen Wagner Harrison seconded Josie's opinion. She'd lost a husband to cancer and raised a son on her own. Until Spence turned up, dazed and bleeding from a car accident, she'd been fighting her own battle with loneliness and near desperation over finances. Her one joy—her only joy—during those dark years was her son. The thought of giving him up, even for his own safekeeping, left her aching for this woman she'd met only once or twice in the past year.

With the quiet competence that characterized her, she deposited an overnight bag on the granite counter. "Spence said you've been holed up here with Luke for going on two days now. I thought you might need a few things. I remembered that we're about the same size.''

''Bless you! As you can see, I've been raiding Luke's closet. I just told him a few minutes ago that I'd have to retrieve some things from my apartment if something doesn't happen soon.''

''Del Brio hasn't made contact?'' Tyler asked sharply. ''Hell, I was sure he would have delivered proof that Lena's okay by now.''

''He did. He e-mailed a photo of her last night, right after you left.''

''Where is it?''

''In my office.''

''Hang loose, I'll get it.''

Tyler was back a few moments later, carrying not just the printed photo but the innocuous-looking device he'd strapped onto Luke's wrist yesterday.

''I found the picture. I also found this on the floor, under your desk.''

''And 'this' is?''

''Sorry. The radar transmitter I brought back yesterday from Fort Hood. Did the strap come loose?''

''No,'' Luke replied with a carefully neutral expression. ''I took it off.''

Haley's face flamed. She remembered exactly when he'd unstrapped the small watchlike device.

Right after its stem had left a sizable scratch on the inside of her right thigh. She'd gathered up the clothes they'd scattered all over the office floor, but had obviously missed the scanner.

Her cheeks hot, she caught Spence's speculative glance. Thankfully the color photo of Lena diverted the keen-eyed former prosecutor's attention. The picture was passed from hand to hand, with the women expressing excitement and relief. The men were more restrained. Flynt and Tyler left it to the lawyer to voice their collective doubts.

"The courts don't accept computer-generated images as evidence for a reason," Spence reminded Luke. "Are you satisfied this one's for real?"

"I e-mailed the photo to some folks in McLean. They say it's genuine."

An almost palpable sense of relief spread through the kitchen.

"All right," Tyler said briskly. "We've cleared the first major hurdle. Now we can concentrate on ransom delivery scenarios. We're pretty well agreed Del Brio's going to insist Haley deliver it in person," he told the women. "We also suspect he wants her as much or more than he wants the cash. Luke as much as told Del Brio he won't get his hands on either his money or his woman."

Incredulous, Marisa swung to the man at her

side. ''And you thought this would make matters easier, Luke?''

''I wasn't trying to make things easier. I was trying to throw Del Brio off balance.''

''Which you did,'' Flynt said dryly. ''You surely did.''

''We'll make sure you knock him more off balance when he comes to collect the money,'' Tyler put in gleefully. ''Ladies, if you want to help, one of you could put on a pot of coffee while—''

''Careful, my dear husband,'' Marisa cooed. ''If you plan to sleep in our bed tonight, you'll consider carefully what you were about to say.''

Blinking, the leather-tough mercenary made a quick recovery. ''What I was about to say, my dear wife, is that one of you ladies could put on a fresh pot while I get more mugs down from the cupboard.''

Making no effort to hide her grin, Ellen volunteered for coffee duty. Soon the scent of rich Colombian blend percolated through the kitchen, and all four couples gathered at the weathered cypress table to strategize possible ransom delivery scenarios.

Three couples, Haley corrected silently as she swept a quick glance around the assembled group. Taciturn Flynt and vivacious Josie so obviously belonged together. As did Spence and his quiet, competent Ellen. Tyler and Marisa struck so many sparks off each other they generated a heat all their own.

She and Luke were the odd ones out. Their tangled pasts had brought everyone else to this place and this time, yet theirs was also the most nebulous relationship. It consisted of one part passion, two parts worry for their daughter, with a large dash of uncertainty thrown in to spice things up even more. Frank wasn't the only one Luke had thrown off balance.

Haley might have decided to put all discussion about last night on ice, but Luke soon discovered his buddies were less reticent. Spence waited only until the four men had walked down to the lake for more practice with the wrist-radar to fall into his prosecuting-attorney mode.

"So what's with you and Haley?"

"Besides a mutual concern for our child? Nothing you need to know about."

"Bull! There was so much electricity between the two of you when we arrived, the air had turned blue. Then there's the matter of that little toy strapped to your wrist. Haley colored up like a Christmas tree when Tyler asked how it got under your desk."

"Come on, Luke," Tyler put in. "Give. How did it get under there?"

"None of your damned business."

Flynt spoke up for the first time. "That's where you're wrong, buddy. It is our business. We're in this all the way with you. And we need to know you won't do something stupid when and if Del Brio makes a grab for Haley."

"Such as?"

"Such as offering yourself as a target in order to get a clean shot at him."

"I'll do whatever it takes to bring him down," Luke said softly, savagely. "Neither Haley nor Lena will be safe until he's out of the picture. Now one of you walk out fifty yards or so and let me get a read on you."

Yesterday afternoon's practice session had provided Luke a general feel for the variations in vibrations the radar returned when it encountered an object. This time he kept all three friends outside in the blazing sun until he was satisfied he could differentiate between their individual radar signatures. As Tyler had reported, the radar was so precise and the vibrations so fine-tuned, Luke should be able to track Del Brio with no difficulty...once he got him away from Lena and Haley.

"You should be okay if only Del Brio shows," Tyler muttered, dragging his forearm across his forehead. "If he brings more than one or two others with him, things could get dicey. Sure you don't want one of us to go along with you?"

"I can't risk it."

Flynt clapped a hand on his shoulder. "We won't be more than a radio call away. I've got my chopper fueled and ready. Once we know the target area, Justin will mobilize his Air Ops Branch. The C.O.'s lined up military air out of Corpus Christi. The FBI's ready to roll. One signal from you, and we're on Del Brio like dirt on a dog."

"The C.O.? You read Colonel Westin in on this?"

"I did. He's flying in this afternoon. Should be here anytime now."

Luke's pulse kicked up a few notches. Once their old commanding officer arrived on the scene, they'd come close to constituting a team again. The only one missing was Ricky Mercado.

"Anyone seen or heard from Ricky since his father was hit?" Luke asked.

"No," Spence replied. "He dropped completely out of sight. My guess is he's either cut his losses and run or he's hunting Del Brio himself."

"There's a third option we have to consider," Luke reminded them. "According to Haley, Frank doesn't trust the son any more than the father. He might have taken Ricky out."

For Haley's sake, he hoped he was wrong. As strong as she was, even Haley might break under the strain of losing another of her family.

The need to protect her blazed fierce and hot. She'd suffered enough. Endured enough. Luke was damned if he'd let anyone hurt her again.

"Move back down to the lake, Spence. I want more practice with this radar unit."

Haley had thought the waiting was bad before. The twenty-four hours following Frank's e-mail left both her nerves and her patience as thin and as brittle as new ice.

The presence of Luke's friends helped. Some. The men refused to display anything but calm confidence. Their wives were warm and supportive. Gradually, Haley got to know the women and they, in turn, came to understand the stress she'd lived with for so many years.

Phillip Westin's arrival late that afternoon provided a welcome distraction. Tall, lean and leathertough, the marine colonel reminded Haley instantly of a middle-aged Clint Eastwood. She couldn't help but notice how his former troops squared their shoulders, sucked in their stomachs and peppered their conversation with "Yes, sir" and "No, sir" whenever they addressed him.

After demanding to know how the heck this bunch of "jar heads" had wound up with such smart, beautiful women, Westin got right down to business. For the rest of the day and a good part of the next, the entire group gathered around the kitchen table, reviewing possible scenarios, postulating potential actions, dissecting every conceivable response.

Frank finally sent the ransom delivery instructions that hot Wednesday evening. They came in the form of another e-mail, short and to the point.

Farm Road 1306.
8.6 miles past intersection with Highway 48.
7 p.m.
Tonight.

"Hell," Tyler muttered, peering over Luke's shoulder. "That's less than an hour from now. You and Haley will have to make tracks to reach the designated rendezvous by seven."

"We'll reach it," Luke vowed. "You guys just take care of the satellite coverage of the area and get the aircraft in the air."

"Will do, buddy." He squeezed his friend's shoulder. "Good luck."

Her heart pounding, Haley accepted a round of fierce hugs from both the men and the women. She couldn't speak, could barely breathe as the team sprang into action like a well-oiled military machine.

Fifteen

Luke's years with OP-12 had taught him that there was only one absolute certainty when it came to field operations.

If something could go wrong, it would.

There was no way to plan for every contingency. No way to account for every variable. Yet he tried to cover as many as possible with Haley during the long, tense drive to the designated site.

"There'll still be some daylight left when we get there. That's good for Frank, not as good for us."

"I know."

"Del Brio may have checkpoints set up. If so, one of his men will pat you down for weapons."

"I know."

Haley stared straight ahead, her palms clammy on the steering wheel of Luke's pickup. The big, heavy truck was dusty, utilitarian and fitted with sheets of steel inside the door panels. Tyler and Flynt had rigged the shields themselves.

"If there's any exchange of fire while we're in

the vehicle, you hit the deck. Got that, Haley? You go down and stay down.''

She dragged her tongue over dry lips. "I've got it.''

"Once we're on the scene, we'll both exit the vehicle. Odds are Frank will instruct you to walk toward him with the briefcase, but you don't take a step until you see Lena. Once we've established her exact position and are sure she's not in the line of fire, you go forward. At an angle.''

"I know.''

"Whatever happens, don't get between me and Del Brio.''

Biting on her lower lip, Haley forced down a rush of hot, bitter nausea. She understood how important it was to maintain a clear field for Luke's radar scanner to pinpoint Frank's position. She also understood that the same clear field gave Frank an unobstructed shot at Luke.

She'd already decided she wouldn't let Frank take that shot. He'd destroyed her family, murdered her mother, almost killed her father. God only knew where her brother was now. She wouldn't, couldn't, let Del Brio destroy Luke, too.

That resolve deepened with every mile the traveled along Farm Road 1306. Sensing how tightly strung she was, Luke had her read the odometer out loud, marking each mile from the turnoff, then every tenth of a mile along the two-lane dirt road.

"Eight point one," she read, wrenching her gaze from the road that cut straight as an arrow through range land dotted with creosote and mesquite.

"Eight point two."

"What time is it?"

"Seven. We're late."

"Just keep going. Tell me what you see."

"Nothing. No cattle. No horses. No houses. Just miles of barbed-wire fence on both sides of the road. Whoever owns this patch of south Texas hasn't put the land to use."

"That's no doubt why Frank chose it. What's the odometer reading?"

"Eight point four."

"Look down the road. See anything?"

"No!" Her stomach roiling, she slowed the truck and read off the last two increments. "Eight point five. Eight point six."

She stood on the brakes. The pickup fishtailed to a stop in the middle of the road.

"There's no one here!"

"Look around. Any hills or trees they could be parked behind, watching our approach?"

Her nerves screaming, she scanned the flat terrain. "No. Nothing bigger than an anthill. All I can see is scrub and— Oh, my God!"

Frantic, she scrabbled for the door handle. Luke wrapped an iron fist around her arm and yanked her down in her seat.

"Talk to me! Tell me what you see."

"There's something caught on the upper strand of the fence just to my left. At first glance, I thought it was a dead animal, but I think... Oh, Luke, I'm sure! It's the stuffed rabbit Lena was holding in the picture Frank e-mailed. And there's a note pinned to it!"

She made another lunge for the door. Once again he hauled her back. "It could be a booby trap."

Instantly sobered, Haley gave him her full attention.

"We'll get out of the truck on my side," he told her. "We take one step at a time. Only one. You'll have to be my eyes."

"Tell me what to look for."

"Depressions in the dirt. Trip wires. A light beam. A pile of grass. Broken creosote branches."

By the time they got within five feet of the stuffed toy, the sleeveless cotton blouse Ellen had brought Haley was damp with sweat. She shook so hard she could barely read the note. "It says to turn right at the next intersection, go twenty-two miles north, head west on 329 to an abandoned farmhouse. We've got thirty minutes to get there."

Luke pushed out a long breath and reached for

the cell phone in his shirt pocket. One click activated the Voice Recognition System and brought his team up on the net.

"Look like Frank is going to send us chasing across half of Texas." Swiftly, he repeated the instructions Haley had just read. "Get a satellite lock on the abandoned farmhouse. We're on the way there now."

Snapping the phone shut, he took Haley's elbow. She should have been the one steering him back to the truck, but he gave her as much or more support than she gave him.

They found another note at the farmhouse, this one directing them to a phone booth at a gas station halfway to San Angelo. Dusk crept across the rolling hills as the pickup sped across Texas. Early stars glowed bright in the lavender sky. Haley didn't spare the sky more than a glance. She kept her eyes on the road ahead and the accelerator hard against the floorboard.

They reached the gas station a good ten minutes ahead of the specified time. Leaving the keys in the ignition, she climbed out and waited for Luke to come around to join her.

"Can you see the booth?"

"Yes."

"Describe it to me."

"It's an open cubicle, with graffiti scrawled all over it. There's no note stuck to it. No note anywhere."

"Go stand on the other side of the truck."

"Why?"

"I want to see if the phone's working."

"You think Frank might have rigged it with explosives?"

"No, I don't. I think he's going to call in a few minutes with more instructions. Just to be safe, though, I want to check out the phone before it rings. Tell me when you're behind the truck."

Haley didn't move. "No, Luke."

"No what?"

"I won't let you take any more risks." Sick with fear for both him and her baby, she fought to keep her voice level. "I shouldn't have come running to you the way I did. I panicked and didn't think things through. I'm the one Frank contacted. I'm the one he wants revenge on. He won't hurt Lena or you if he has me."

"Yeah, well, what Frank wants and what he gets are—"

"Listen to me, Luke. I'm telling you there's been a change in tactics. If Frank is planning a snatch and run, as you and Tyler and the others seem to think, I intend to let him know right up front that I'll go with him voluntarily. My only condition is that he leaves Lena with you."

She expected him to get all macho and blast her with a dozen different arguments. Instead, he folded his arms and let the summer night swirl hot and dusty around them.

"Just out of curiosity, when did you decide on this change in tactics?"

"A while ago."

"When, Haley?"

"Look, it's been building inside me for the past couple days, okay? The guilt. The fear. The worry that I've dragged you into the same pit my family got dragged into. I can't do it, Luke. I can't let Frank destroy you, too."

"It's been building inside me, too," he said quietly. "The guilt because I wasn't there when you and Lena needed me. The fear that I can't protect either of you. The worry that I might lose you again."

Trailing his knuckles along her cheek until he found her nape, he pulled her forward.

"I'm breaking all the rules here, Haley. This isn't the time or the place for this. But yesterday morning, when it didn't seem to matter to you that I might never fully regain my sight, it made me think... Made me realize... Oh, hell, I'm not any good at this."

Haley's pulse tripped. For a moment the dust-streaked glass of the phone booth blurred. The stars faded. The night sky became a backdrop. Her entire being focused on the man standing in front of her.

"Any good at what?"

"Telling a woman that I love her."

When she didn't answer, a small, wry smile played at one corner of his mouth.

"Like I said, I'm breaking all the rules here. The last thing I should do is add to your stress. I don't expect you to feel the same. Nor do I expect you to think about this right now. I just want you to understand why I can't step aside and let you do this alone."

She stood silent for so long, Luke figured she'd taken him at his word and decided not to think about anything but Lena.

"You're right," she said at last. "This isn't the time or the place for this, but we might not get another. I love you, too, Luke. I've loved you since I was old enough to figure out what Barbie and Ken were up to when they closed the door to her Dream House. You don't have any idea how many times I padded my bras to get you to notice me. Or how many nights I went to bed almost screaming with frustration when you didn't."

"I noticed, sweetheart. Believe me, I noticed. But you were Ricky's sister and I..."

"I know. You wouldn't cross the line. I did, though. Too many times. I ached for you so much I had to steal one more hour with you that awful night on the lake. I was the one who suggested we go out back at the Saddlebag. I was thrilled when I found out I was pregnant. Knowing my baby would have some of you in her made her doubly precious to me."

Luke was humbled. Completely humbled. Cupping her cheeks, he bent to express his feelings in the surest, most direct way he knew. The phone jangled before he could do more than graze her lips.

Cursing, he thrust Haley away. "Get around to the other side of the truck."

"Luke, wait!"

Ignoring her cry, he followed the sound and wrapped his fist around the receiver. "Tell me when you're in position."

The phone shrilled again.

"Move, Haley. If it rings too many times, he'll get suspicious."

He heard her take one step, then hesitate. Another jangle cut through the night.

"Move!"

She stomped around to the far side of the pickup, and Luke snatched up the receiver.

Luke made the last leg of their journey blind. Literally and figuratively. The road Del Brio directed them to was another two-lane dirt track, with no streetlights to provide enough contrast for Luke to see so much as a shadow. And this time they hadn't been given any instructions about how far to go. They could keep going, Del Brio had sneered, until they were stopped.

The first clue that they were approaching the rendezvous point came via secure radio/phone net.

"The military LanSat network picked up three stationary vehicles," Colonel Westin reported crisply. "They're in a triangular vector approximately five miles north, six west, and five-point-four south-southeast of your present position."

"Roger that."

"Given your heading and the condition of the road, we estimate you'll make contact with the vehicle to the west of you in about ten minutes."

"Ten minutes. Got it."

"We'll be just over the horizon. Good hunting, Luke."

"Thanks, Colonel."

Snapping the lid down on the phone, he tucked it in his shirt pocket and activated the miniaturized scanner on his left wrist. The titanium case vibrated violently as the radar wave it sent out bounced off the dash. His nerves dancing in response, Luke raised his arm and aimed the scanner at the windshield. The vibrations died instantly.

Satisfied that there was nothing out there for the radar to pick up, he reached into his boot and slid the snubnose .38 from its ankle holster. Staring into the darkness, he released the cylinder, ran his thumb around the six chambered rounds and closed the weapon with a small snick. He would have preferred the SIG Sauer 9 mm Tyler had fitted with a special scope. After testing several different ways to conceal it, however, he'd opted for the smaller Smith & Wesson.

"We should make contact within the next few minutes."

Her response was quick and gritty. "I'm ready."

"We're a team, remember? We're in this together. I want you to promise you won't deliberately place yourself in the line of fire."

"Luke, I—"

"I can't risk a shot unless I know you and the baby are clear," he said fiercely. "Don't give him any more advantage than he already has. Promise me, Haley."

"All right, all right! I promise."

* * *

That pledge thundered in Haley's mind when she topped a small rise a few moments later and drove smack into a blaze of light. With a smothered oath, she stomped on the brakes.

Luke was right there beside her, calm but urgent. "What do you see?"

"There's a vehicle parked smack in the middle of the road approximately twenty yards ahead. Its high beams are on. The damned things almost blinded me."

"Just maneuver the bastard in front of those lights," Luke said on a note of triumph, "and I won't need any high-tech scanners to get him in my sights."

His utter confidence gave Haley a badly needed shot in the arm. Maybe, just maybe, they might pull this off. She was shaking when she reached behind her for the ransom money, but not completely mindless with terror.

"Remember the drill," Luke cautioned as she tugged on the door handle. "We get out together. You stay left. I stay right. Don't take one step until Del Brio produces Lena."

"I've got it."

"Here we go."

Shouldering open the heavy, reinforced door, Haley emerged into the hot Texas night. She heard the passenger door slam shut, but couldn't see a thing in the glare of the headlights. The thought flashed into her head that she and Luke had reversed roles. The blazing lights blinded her, but would provide just the contrast he needed to make out Frank's silhouette. Assuming they could get Del Brio to step in front of his car, that was.

"Frank?" Holding up her arm to shield her eyes, she squinted at the other vehicle. "Frank, are you there?"

His chuckle floated to her through the night. "I'm here, babe."

The sound of his voice twisted Haley into knots.

"I see you brought the money," he called. "Callaghan, too. Keep your hands where I can see 'em, both of you." His laugh twisted into a sneer. "Not that I need to worry about you, do I, Callaghan? I ought to blow a hole in you right now, you useless son of a bitch, and put you out of your misery."

Afraid he'd do just that, Haley rushed into an explanation. "Luke came along because of Lena. He provided the money for her ransom. He just wants to make sure she's okay."

"That right, rich boy? You just want to check on your brat? Well, I guess I can let you have a look." Snickering at his cruel joke, he raised his voice. "Bring her out, Erica."

A healthy chunk of Haley's hate for Frank Del Brio took an instant detour into fury.

Erica. He could only mean Erica Clawson.

Haley had worked with the short, carrot-topped waitress for more than a year. Although she hadn't gotten close to anyone except Ginger Walton, the one friend she'd made as Daisy Parker, she'd fretted when Erica gushed about her new boyfriend, yet came to work with bruises and, once, a black eye.

She tried to coax the younger woman into talking to a counselor, but didn't want to get too close, reveal too much of herself. Then Lena had been kidnapped from Flynt's ranch, and Erica Clawson dropped instantly from Haley's list of worries.

Dammit all to hell! Why hadn't she seen beyond the waitress's appearance? Why hadn't she connected Erica's mysterious, ready-fisted boyfriend with Frank Del Brio? The FBI hadn't made the connection, either, but that didn't lessen Haley's biting self-disgust.

"You want to see your kid, Callaghan?" Frank's laughter rolled through the night again. "Here she is."

A lump the size of a Texas armadillo lodged in Haley's throat as a tall, muscled figure moved into the spear of lights. She didn't have to fake her quaver of fear when she called out to Del Brio.

"We can't see anything from here. You're just a dark blur."

"Come take a look. Bring the money."

She took one step, heard Luke's hiss and stopped. "No. I'm not delivering the money until I know Lena's all right. Bring her halfway, Frank, then step back."

"Aw, babe. It's breakin' my heart you don't trust me."

The words came out playfully enough, but Del Brio's real feelings broke through as he picked up the carrier and sauntered forward.

"Just like it broke my heart you didn't trust me all those years ago when we were engaged. I would've taken care of you, Haley. I would have covered for your father. Why did you run? Why did you leave me thinking you were dead?"

She could feel his anger. It swept across the blaze of lights in palpable waves. She could feel the hurt, as well. In his own sick way, he'd loved her. Her flesh crawled when he made it plain he still did.

"I've been wondering what you did with your ring," he called.

"I lost it in the lake, Frank." No way she was going to tip him over the edge by admitting she'd thrown it as far away as she could. Not when she was this close to Lena.

"Never mind. I'll buy you another one. Bigger. Flashier. This time we'll do it right, Haley. When I put it on your finger, you won't want to take it off."

"Frank!"

Erica Clawson's shriek split the night.

"What's this crap about putting a ring on that bitch's finger? You promised to marry me!"

Erica charged out of the darkness and was met with a lash of scorn.

"Don't be stupid. Why would I marry a slut like you? You spread your legs for me, you'll spread 'em for anyone in pants."

"Me? You're calling me a slut?" Her outrage piled on top of anguish. "What about Princess Daisy here? She's the one who spread her legs. You're holding the evidence of that in your hand."

"Haley made a mistake," Frank snarled. "You, you're nothing but a tramp."

"Tramp! I'll show you tramp!"

Her hands curled into claws, Erica launched herself at Frank. He whirled to meet her, one arm swinging the baby carrier in a wide arc, the aiming a dark shape that could only be a gun at Erica's heart.

Haley didn't stop to think. Didn't give a single consideration as to whether she was putting herself between Frank and Luke. She hurtled forward at the same instant Del Brio fired.

Knocking the carrier out of his hand, Haley came down on top of the hard plastic. With a small, stunned cry, Erica came down on top of her. Frantically, Haley stooped over the carrier, shielding it with her body.

She heard more shots. Two. Three.

A hoarse shout.

Someone called her name.

Drenched in Erica's blood, hunched like a crab over her baby, her ears ringing from the shock waves of Frank's pistol fired at close range, she prayed that someone was Luke.

It wasn't.

It was her brother.

She recognized his voice finally, after his frantic hands pulled Erica's lifeless body away and the reverberations in her ear died enough for her to hear.

"Haley! Dear God, Haley, are you hurt?"

Dazed, she abandoned her protective crouch and raised up on her knees. Her stomach lurched when she spotted Frank Del Brio lying facedown only a few yards from Erica's lifeless body. It took another dive when she looked into the face of the man standing over her.

"Ricky?"

"Yeah, it's me." Hunkering beside her, he gathered her into his arms. "I thought I'd lost you. I thought I'd lost both you and Lena."

Lena! Dear God, Lena!

Only then did a series of indignant squalls pierce the clanging in Haley's ears. Shoving out of her brother's arms, she righted the overturned carrier.

Her face brick-red, Lena waved her fists in the air and let everyone in south Texas know that she was very unhappy. Haley's eyes brimmed with tears as she fumbled with the straps, pulled her baby from the carrier and dropped a kiss on her curls. Lena tight in her arms, Haley swung to face her brother.

"Ricky, where's Luke?"

The frantic question no sooner tumbled out than Luke himself answered.

"I'm right here."

He stepped out of the darkness into the arc thrown by the headlights. With a small cry, Haley rushed to him. The acrid stench of gunpowder clung to his shirt. She had no idea whether he'd fired the shots that brought Frank down, and didn't care. The only thing that mattered was that he was safe. He and Lena.

The baby's squalls didn't lessen in either volume or intensity as Haley held out the bundle of flailing arms and legs.

"Meet your daughter, Mr. Callaghan."

Epilogue

It was a perfect day for a wedding, Texas-style.

The summer sun floated in a cloudless sky. Heat rose in shimmering waves from the manicured fairways of the Lone Star Country Club. The assembled guests weren't worried about patches of unsightly sweat staining their pastel tea gowns and dove-gray morning coats, however. Giant fans discreetly positioned behind hedges blew cool, refreshing mists.

Most of Mission Creek, including the influential Carsons and Wainwrights, had gathered under the bright sun. Old feuds forgotten, the long-divided families intermingled in row after row of white-skirted chairs. Colonel Phillip Westin sat in the front row, stiff-backed and square-jawed in his dress blues, his medals gleaming in the sun. Next to the colonel sat Teresa Chavez, who picked her husband's pocket for a dry handkerchief to replace the one she'd already soaked.

"It's so beautiful," she murmured, dabbing her eyes. "All these roses."

It seemed as though every hothouse in south Texas had been raided. Garlands of yellow roses were draped between the rows. White netting entwined with thousands of the same fragrant blossoms festooned the patio where the reception would be held. Hundreds more climbed the arch that had been hastily constructed over the tee box of hole number nine.

Five men stood under the arch. Tall. Tanned. Shoulder to shoulder. At their feet, squarely in the center of the raised platform, was a baby carrier. A toddler with a lacy elastic headband holding back her black curls waved her arms and legs and blew happy bubbles into the air.

Hooking a hand in his white tie, one of Lena's honorary uncles glanced around the elegant scene and grinned. "I still can't believe your woman decided to make things official here on the golf course, Callaghan."

"Believe it, Murdoch."

"We heard you had to sign a promise in blood that you'd show this time," Spence drawled.

"I would've used a pen," Luke tossed back, "but Lena had just tried out her new back teeth on my finger. The ink ran a little red."

"Well, I think holding the ceremony out here makes perfect sense," Flynt murmured. "This is where it all began."

Not quite, Luke thought. It began years ago, with a gawky teenager who blossomed into a lush, beautiful woman and a hardheaded Texan who put friendship ahead of his growing hunger.

Luke didn't turn his head or try to focus the blurred images that were becoming a little sharper each day. He knew his best man stood beside him, as he'd stood beside him so many times in the past.

Luke and Ricky had recovered a lot of ground since the night they took down Frank Del Brio. According to the coroner, it was anyone's guess whether Del Brio died from the bullet through his heart or through his brain.

Neither Luke nor Ricky particularly cared. Del Brio was out of the picture. Haley and Lena were safe. The FBI had come through with their promise of immunity for Ricky and Johnny Mercado. The band of brothers stood together again.

All was right with the world, Luke decided. But he didn't have any idea how right until a rustle of movement swept through the guests. Luke heard a few excited murmurs. A moment later the organist hit a loud chord and Mendelssohn's glorious "Wedding March" pumped into the air.

"Here we go." Ricky's murmur reached him over the swelling notes. "You ready, pal?"

"Just keep that ring handy."

A swish of skirts announced the arrival of

Haley's maid of honor. Ginger Walton Turner had wanted Daisy Parker to perform the same service at her wedding a few months ago. Haley hadn't dared risk the exposure then. Today the two friends could both bask in their happiness.

Three bridesmaids followed Ginger along the petal-strewn carpet to the tee box. Ellen Harrison, Josie Carson and Marisa Murdoch took their places beside Ginger.

Suddenly the organist put all she had into the equivalent of a drumroll. The notes rose higher, louder, startling a cry from Lena. Five men bent toward the infant. With a sheepish grin, four stepped back.

Luke straightened a moment later. With his daughter nestled in the crook of his arm, he stood tall and waited for Haley. She came down the aisle slowly, matching her pace to her father's. Only days out of the hospital, Johnny Mercado still moved cautiously, but both father and daughter were serenely oblivious of the gasps of astonishment that rose when they appeared.

"She's wearing red!" Luke heard someone exclaim.

Not any red. Hot, chili-pepper red. Red gown. Red shoes. Red roses wreathed in her hair. She'd worn it for Luke, so he could see the haze of bright color silhouetted against the white chairs and miles of netting. So he could see his bride.

He hadn't thought that he could love her any more than he already did, but his heart swelled at that glorious blaze. His heart swelling, he stepped down to take her hand from her father's.

"Couldn't you leave that child in her carrier for a half hour?" she asked, laughing.

"Nope." Hitching Lena up higher, he escorted his women back to the platform. "Any more than I can leave her behind when we take off on our honeymoon."

"Which begs the question," Haley murmured as the music swelled to a final crescendo, "where are we going?"

"You pick it. The Caribbean. Hawaii. Europe."

"I'd like to go back to London. We left in such a hurry, I never said goodbye to my friends."

The music died. The minister stepped forward. Luke cut him off before he got out more than "Dearly Beloved."

"Hang on a minute, will you, padre?"

Startled, the minister looked to the best man, who shook his head. The guests exchanged equally confused glances as Luke smiled down at the pale, blurred oval of Haley's face.

"We can go anywhere you want, my darling,

whenever you want, as long as we come home once in a while.''

More astonished gasps rose from the guests as the bride threw her arms around her not-quite-yet husband's neck.

''I am home. For good this time. It's you and Texas, Luke. Now and forever.''

''That's all I wanted to hear, sweetheart.''

He bent toward her, provoking an amused observation from the minister. ''The kiss usually comes after the vows, you know.''

''Not this time, padre.''

Glorying in the love that radiated from the woman in red, Luke wrapped his free arm around her waist. As he pulled Haley up against him, Lena laughed in delight and patted him on the cheek.

* * * * *

*You will love the next story from
Silhouette's*
LONE STAR COUNTRY CLUB:
HER SWEET TALKIN' MAN
by Myrna Mackenzie

*Available September 2002 (at Direct
only)*

*Turn the page for an excerpt from this
exciting romance...!*

One

"**W**hoa, this is going to be some family reunion. Especially since the rest of the Carson family doesn't even know you exist," Ace Turner Carson told himself as he pulled his white sedan into the aboveground parking garage of the Mission Creek Memorial Hospital.

No surprise since *he* hadn't even know his true roots until three months ago when his mother had died.

But now he knew. Things he almost wished he didn't know, he thought with a grimace. And he had had to take the next step and come to Mission Creek, Texas. His mother had suffered years of humiliation and pain after she'd been abandoned by the man she loved. For Carson deserved to suffer a little humiliation in kind.

Who better to engineer that than a hell-raising bad seed of an unwanted son?

"So bring on the family reunion," Ace whispered. "And let's make it as public an event as possible. Past time to get in the dance, buddy."

Besides, Ace had to admit this could be fun—
in spite of all his misgivings about even being in
this unfamiliar town where the wealthy Carsons
had so much influence, in spite of his reluctance
to even meet the man who had given him life. He
nodded and smiled. Could be real fun. Especially
if he hammed things up a bit, exaggerated things,
really worked hard at being an embarrassment to
his dear old dad.

"Oh, yes, this is going to involve some intense
concentration, Carson. Some single-minded devo-
tion."

Which was why when a tiny, well-curved redhead entered his field of vision making a beeline
to the parking garage elevator, Ace ignored his au-
tomatic response to her undeniably appealing little
body. He told himself "no."

"No distractions," he reminded himself. "You
came here for a reason."

Yes, but that didn't mean he'd gone completely
numb to the world and blind to the things that
made a man a man and a woman a woman. He
might be on a single-minded quest, but this was no
ordinary woman. And after all, he wasn't going to
do anything but look, anyway. And maybe flirt—
just a bit. An elevator ride didn't leave a man time
for much more.

As she moved nearer and scanned her surroundings, clearly on the alert for thugs and wolves on the prowl, the redhead revealed wide hazel eyes that still held a hint of innocence in spite of the fact that she appeared to be in her early thirties. Interesting. What was even more interesting was that underneath her knee-length, ice-blue suit a pair of the finest legs ever to grace Texas or even the planet were on display. Her hair was a mass of silk held back with silver clips. The strands practically begged for a man to unsnap those clips and sift through the silk with his fingertips.

Of course, touching her was absolutely out of the question. He wanted to admire her, not distress her. So, when an elderly couple turned down the aisle on their way to the elevator, too, Ace grinned at them and moved forward. The beauty would know she was safe now.

He sauntered toward the elevator, his long legs taking him there ahead of her.

"Allow me to get that for you, darlin'," he said, stepping forward to push the elevator button. "Looks like your hands are full."

The lady stopped in her tracks. She reached out for the button at the same moment he had, and she looked down at his hand, which was just over her own. Her skin nearly met his. He could feel her warmth. he could feel something else radiating from her. Awareness?

"Thank you, sir," she said, "but I think you're mistaken about my inability to handle such a simple task. After all, my hands aren't nearly full. I'm only carrying a clipboard. And I'm truly sorry, but I don't *ever* answer to the name 'darlin'.'"

He raised a brow because, after all, she *had* just answered.

A slight blush turned her cheeks an endearing rose as she realized her mistake. And did he say that her eyes held a trace of innocence? Well, yes, they did, but they could also flash intense green sparks when she was perturbed. She appeared to be pretty darn perturbed right now, like a kitten that suddenly remembered it had lionesses for relatives.

Ace couldn't help smiling at the thought—and he couldn't help being intrigued. That blush and those eyes told him she hadn't had much experience with men like himself who blatantly spoke their minds or didn't bother hiding their interest. But she didn't back away. Her hair swung back when she dared to look up and stare him straight in the eye. That was fortunate for him, since the movement exposed a neck that was long and pretty and pale. She had little, delicate earlobes that made him dream of nibbling that tender spot just beneath her ear to see if he could make her sigh and gasp.

His entire body responded to the thought, and that overly intense reaction gave him pleasure.

Careful, buddy, he warned himself. Easy. She hadn't revealed her skin on purpose and would no doubt be appalled if she knew that the neat little collar of her suit made him think of peeling back the lapels and letting his fingers brush her flesh. She was obviously a by-the-book, never-break-the-rules lady and he was a prowling alley cat, a man who never, ever touched a woman who hadn't been born a little wild and who liked things that way. Seeing how things were, he should probably just apologize and call the game off.

"You're right. I misspoke. Excuse me," he said, as the elderly couple and the elevator arrived and he motioned everyone in ahead of him with a slight bow.

But then he stepped in behind the red-haired beauty and the orange blossom scent of her slipped in and caught him unaware. Nothing like the enticing scent of a lovely woman to play havoc with a man's good intentions.

The secret is out!

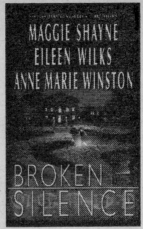

Coming in May 2003 to SILHOUETTE BOOKS

Evidence has finally surfaced that a covert team
of scientists successfully completed experiments
in genetic manipulation.

The extraordinary individuals created by these
experiments could be anyone, living anywhere,
even right next door....

Enjoy these three brand-new FAMILY SECRETS
stories and watch as dark pasts are exposed
and passion burns through the night!

The Invisible Virgin by Maggie Shayne
A Matter of Duty by Eileen Wilks
Inviting Trouble by Anne Marie Winston

Five extraordinary siblings. One dangerous past.

Where love comes alive™

LONE STAR
LSCC
COUNTRY CLUB
EST. 1923

Where Texas society reigns supreme—and appearances are *everything!*

Collect three (3) original proofs of purchase from the back pages of three (3) Lone Star Country Club titles and receive a free Lone Star book (regularly retailing at $4.75 U.S./$5.75 CAN.) that's not yet available in retail outlets!

Just complete the order form and send it, along with three (3) proofs of purchase from three (3) different Lone Star titles to: Lone Star Country Club, P.O. Box 9047, Buffalo, NY 14269-9047, or P.O. Box 613, Fort Erie, Ontario L2A 5X3.

----

093 KJH DNC3

_____

Name (PLEASE PRINT)

_____

Address   Apt. #

_____

City   State/Prov.   Zip/Postal Code

Please specify which title(s) you would like to receive:

❏   0-373-61364-4   *Her Sweet Talkin' Man*
❏   0-373-61365-2   *Mission Creek Mother-To-Be*
❏   0-373-61366-0   *The Lawman*
❏   0-373-61367-9   *Doctor Seduction*

❏ Have you enclosed your proofs of purchase?

Remember—for each title selected, you must send three (3) original proofs of purchase. To receive all four (4) titles, just send in twelve (12) proofs of purchase, one from each of the 12 Lone Star Country Club titles.

LONE STAR
LSCC
COUNTRY CLUB
EST. 1923

One Proof of Purchase
LSCCPOP12

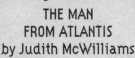

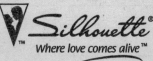